"What if we pretend

He saw her eyes flare wide in surprise.

"Hear me out," he said. "I could help you learn how to talk to guys."

She whirled on him. "Why me?" she demanded.

He ran a sheepish hand through his hair. "You're the only person I know in town." Wrong answer. He knew it as soon as the words left his mouth. Whatever tiny spark of interest he'd thought he'd seen in her eyes was extinguished.

"Do you really want to keep hiding behind store displays? Wishing for the courage to go up and talk to somebody you like?"

She quickly swiped beneath her eye. Was she crying?

"Look, I'm sorry," he said. "I didn't mean to hurt your feelings. I thought maybe we could help each other."

She wasn't walking away... Did that mean she was considering his offer?

It shouldn't matter to him. *She* shouldn't matter.

She gave a slight nod. And then she turned and walked on.

What did it mean? *I'll do it?*

Lucy Bayer writes Amish novels from her home in the Midwest. She is a mother of four and an avid birder.

Books by Lucy Bayer

Love Inspired

A Convenient Amish Bride
Their Forbidden Amish Match
Their Secret Amish Arrangement

Visit the Author Profile page at LoveInspired.com.

Their Secret Amish Arrangement

LUCY BAYER

LOVE INSPIRED

INSPIRATIONAL ROMANCE

LOVE INSPIRED®

INSPIRATIONAL ROMANCE

ISBN-13: 978-1-335-59739-7

Their Secret Amish Arrangement

Copyright © 2024 by Lacy Williams

Love Inspired
22 Adelaide St. West, 41st Floor
Toronto, Ontario M5H 4E3, Canada
www.LoveInspired.com

Printed in Lithuania

MIX
Paper | Supporting responsible forestry
FSC® C021394

Let all your things be done with charity.
—*1 Corinthians* 16:14

Chapter One

Henry Barrett stared at the mess, fuming.

There was graffiti on the living room wall. Graffiti that hadn't been there three days ago, when he'd done a final walk-through with Dad before his father had closed on the house.

A glance beyond the living room showed glass shattered on the kitchen floor. Someone had broken in. Kids? Whoever the troublemaker was, they'd created more work for Henry. Now he would have to board up the window. Replace the glass.

It could add an entire day to his already-tight schedule. He needed to renovate this house in two months to meet the deadline Dad had set for this project. His father owned a business that bought and flipped houses and Henry had worked with Dad since he was a junior in high school.

Dad had laid out the plans for this house, including re-texturing and painting the walls, but would it take extra primer to cover the deep red spray paint?

He scowled.

He pulled his cell phone out of his pocket, ready to call his brother Todd and vent some of his frustration. Not Dad. Dad was trusting him with this job. And he needed to prove himself after the last failure.

Todd had changed his whole life earlier this year. Henry's big-city doctor brother had left behind the ER job at Barrett Lakeview Hospital in Columbus, Ohio, and instead taken over the small-town general practice here in Hickory Harbor.

Todd loved it here. He sang the town's praises. Made it sound almost idyllic. But perfect towns didn't have break-ins.

At the last second, Henry froze with his hand on his phone. He couldn't call or text his brother. When Todd had moved, he'd also joined the Amish church, which meant giving up technology. Like his cell phone. And his beloved car.

Sometimes, Henry still couldn't believe it.

He dialed the nonemergency line for the police instead of calling Todd.

They promised to send an officer over.

Henry hoped the officer arrived soon. He couldn't afford to lose a day of work but needed to document this for insurance purposes.

Walking past the living room and down the hall toward the bedrooms, he prayed he wasn't going to find more damage.

He'd written a list of everything he was going to renovate in this single-story farmhouse. Rip up the carpets and put in hardwood flooring. Scrape the ceilings, which still had the popcorn texture from forty years ago. Retexture everything. Paint every wall in the place. Henry was going to make the biggest changes in the kitchen. Kitchens happened to be his specialty.

But first, he had to get all this garbage cleared out.

He'd had a huge metal trash container delivered to the driveway. Now he just needed to fill it up with all the junk.

Who would leave a house in this poor condition?

Henry kicked at a piece of debris in the hallway with his steel-toed work boot. Old clothes. Pizza boxes. A disgusting mattress in one of the bedrooms. Broken children's toys. Crumpled paper.

There was trash everywhere.

That's what happened sometimes when a house went to auction. The previous tenants trashed it.

And it wasn't fun to be the new owner and have to clean it up.

Henry had hired someone from a local cleaning company to come out and help him for the day.

With two bodies filling up trash bags and hauling trash, they'd get through the mess in no time.

He hoped.

"Hello?" a timid female voice called out from the other end of the house.

Was that his cleaner? He would've expected a police officer to have a more strident voice, so it probably was.

He strode out of the farthest bedroom and down the hall. He found her just inside the front door.

She was indeed carrying a caddy of cleaning supplies, but the young woman standing gingerly on the threshold—and staring in dismay at the wreck of a house—wasn't what he'd expected.

She was Amish.

She wore a pale blue dress that went down to touch her tennis shoes. A long white apron covered the front of the dress. She had hazel eyes and her dark hair was pulled up behind her head and covered in one of the white head coverings he'd seen on other Amish women.

She was fresh-faced and looked barely old enough to be eighteen.

This was who the cleaning company had sent him?

Her startled gaze collided with his stare and she recoiled slightly, looking like she might run away. Probably because of the scowl he could feel twisting his lips.

"I'm from the cleaning company," she said faintly. The words were barely a breath.

Was she shy or had he frightened her?

He held up his hands in front of him to show he wasn't a danger. "I'm Henry Barrett. I'm the one who called the cleaning company." He shook his head. "There must've been some mistake."

He had been sure he'd called a non-Amish company. He'd even checked their website for references. Amish people didn't use computers and such, did they?

He didn't actually know a lot about the Amish people in Hickory Harbor. Todd was the one who'd been interested, ever since they'd discovered they had a long-lost brother who'd been raised here. Raised Amish.

Henry didn't care to know.

But now his inattention might cost him.

He sighed. "I told the company it wasn't going to be dusting and cleaning windows and such. I need someone to help me bag up all this trash and haul it out to the dumpster."

He saw her scan the floor, register how much work it was going to be. It would take all day.

She still didn't say anything. She'd barely said two words since she'd arrived.

"I'm going to call the company," he muttered, reaching for his cell phone a second time. "Ask them to send someone—" he gestured to her without really looking "—else."

She really did look like she'd blow away if pushed by a brisk wind. He needed someone with a strong back.

Before he could find the website and phone number for

the cleaning company, he heard the crunch of tires on gravel and a car shut off.

A glance out the window confirmed it was a uniformed police officer. The young woman—he realized he hadn't even got her name—scurried a few steps inside, out of the doorway.

He figured he'd deal with her after he made his police report. What a mess. He already felt behind and now he was going to have to sort out the cleaner.

Henry met the officer outside and gave him his statement. They walked around the outside of the house together, and Henry was dismayed to see that graffiti covered the side of the small barn at the end of the driveway behind the house, too. The barn was in good condition and he didn't want to replace any of the walls. It was an expense he didn't need. He'd have to scrub off the spray paint.

It was another mark on the day that made his mood even blacker.

The officer asked whether he could walk through the house and Henry allowed it, standing next to his truck as he tried to gather his thoughts.

He rubbed one hand through his hair, frustration mounting. Dad was counting on him, had given him a second chance.

He wasn't going to let a couple of setbacks ruin this for him.

The police cruiser pulled away and Henry went inside to tell the cleaner that she wasn't needed.

He didn't see her when he walked inside, but there was noise coming from one of the back bedrooms. When Henry passed by the kitchen, he saw her caddy with cleaning supplies on the counter. Next to it was a small brown bag. Her lunch, he assumed.

He found her in the farthest bedroom. She'd grabbed a black trash bag—he didn't know where she'd gotten it—and already filled it half-full.

Henry stood there in surprise for a moment as she kept scooping up more trash to put inside.

Clara Templeton felt her face heat as she registered the presence of the *Englisher* man from the doorway.

Henry Barrett.

He'd given her his name, but she'd found herself tongue-tied and hadn't given hers.

This is a mistake.

She pretended to ignore him as his words from earlier played in her brain.

It was eerily similar to something Great-Aunt Dorcas would've said and Clara's instant reaction was a desire to prove him wrong.

She gingerly picked up what might've once been a sweatshirt but was stained and ripped until it was unrecognizable. Underneath was a broken glass bottle, pieces of it ground into the ugly carpet under her feet.

"Stop."

Henry Barrett's barked command made her freeze, clutching the trash bag in her hands. Her eyes went to him, unbidden.

He was angry. Or frustrated maybe.

And handsome.

Wait. Was she supposed to think such things? Even after two years, she was still learning the ways of the Amish. Clara knew that it was a sin to be vain, to care too much about her own appearance. Was it also a sin to admire someone else's?

He was pleasing, she amended internally. He had dark hair and blue eyes, tanned skin that made her think he spent a lot of time out in the sun, and a chiseled jaw that was covered in two days of stubble.

Right now, a muscle in that jaw was ticking. He crossed his arms over his chest and she realized she'd been staring without saying anything.

A blush scorched its way up her neck and into her face.

"I was planning to call your company and ask for a replacement."

"Please don't." She whispered the words before she realized the way he'd phrased it. *I was planning...*

"I'm a hard worker," she said quickly, when the silence stretched beyond a moment. Her tongue felt as if it was glued to the roof of her mouth and she couldn't seem to raise her voice above a whisper. "I can clean all this up." She waved her hand vaguely. There was trash everywhere.

He sighed. "How old are you?"

Does that matter? The words popped into her brain but she swallowed them. *Don't sass.* That was her late grandmother's voice and it stuck in her memory like a fingerprint on a newly-scrubbed window.

"I'm twenty-three," she said.

Something glinted in his eyes. Maybe surprise. She'd been told she looked younger than her actual age. She didn't see why it mattered. Eighteen or twenty-three, this job needed to be done, and she was here.

She started to squat down and reach for the broken bottle.

"Hold on," Henry snapped.

He was certainly bossy.

"I've got an extra pair of gloves in my toolbox. In the truck," he added.

He seemed to want her to follow him, so she left the trash bag behind and trailed him out of the house into the bright morning sunlight. He was muttering to himself, but she couldn't make out the words.

She swallowed back a half dozen questions. Was this his house? Was it a case of bad renters who'd trashed the place? Or had he bought it like this? She racked her brain and thought she remembered a for-sale sign out in front of the yard recently. Why would someone buy a house in such terrible condition?

She didn't ask any of the questions tumbling through her mind.

Grandmother Mildred and Grandfather Titus had wanted a little girl who would be seen and not heard.

When she'd arrived on their doorstep after a terrible car accident had taken the lives of her mom and dad, Clara had been lost and alone. And full of questions.

And her paternal grandparents hadn't been equipped to nurture a six-year-old. She'd learned quickly that asking too many questions or being too loud in general would result in her being sent to her room.

She'd been schooled at home from that time and worked on the small farm they owned. She'd been isolated and lonely.

And her shy nature had grown and grown.

It hadn't gotten any better when she'd been forced to move in with Great-Aunt Dorcas.

She hung back as Henry Barrett rifled through the toolbox in the bed of his truck.

"Where'd you come from?" he asked.

What?

"There's no buggy," he continued over his shoulder when she didn't answer.

Did he think all Amish people drove a buggy?

She cleared her throat. "I walked."

He turned to her, a pair of leather gloves in his extended hand. His eyes darted to the sky and back. "It's cold out," he murmured. Then, "What's your name?"

"Clara Templeton."

"Clara." Her name sounded different somehow, the way it rolled off his tongue. The blush that hadn't seemed to leave her face all morning burned even hotter.

"I guess we're working together today, Clara." He didn't sound thrilled about the prospect. "Please be careful. I saw that broken bottle. There may be other things you could cut yourself on. I'd rather you let me handle anything dangerous or heavy."

That was…thoughtful. When was the last time someone had been protective of her? She couldn't remember. She knew he was probably only saying what he'd said because of liability. He didn't want to have to pay for a doctor's visit. But it was still nice.

She took the gloves. "Thank you."

He sighed again.

She had heard sighs like that like for as long as she could remember. It was a sound that meant her presence wasn't wanted. That she was doing some chore wrong. Or that she should go away.

Usually a sigh like that made her want to run and hide. But right now, a different feeling filled her. She could do this job. And she wanted to prove it.

She took the gloves and went back inside the house. She started filling the trash bag. And then a second one, once the first was bulging and full.

She didn't know Henry Barrett. He didn't know her. But she needed the money from today's job, and maybe it was a culmination of everything she'd been through in the past twenty-six months.

She needed to do a good job.

Her back and arms were aching from hauling the bags of trash to the dumpster on the driveway by lunchtime. It took her two tries to ask Henry Barrett if she could take a short break to eat the sack lunch she'd brought with her.

He waved her off from extracting a toilet that had been broken from the floor. She took that as permission.

She went outside and sat on the front stoop, thankful for the brisk autumn breeze and a break from the stale, dirty air inside.

All morning long, she'd heard sounds from inside the walls concentrated at the back corner of the house. She thought it was mice.

As she ate her peanut butter and jelly sandwich, she heard rustling beneath the same corner of the house.

She looked over to see a hole in the wood board that covered the crawl space. That must be where the mice were getting in.

She hadn't told Henry Barrett. She figured he would hear the noises himself.

Finished with her sandwich, she tossed her unpeeled orange between her hands. Something moved under the corner of the house.

That was definitely bigger than a mouse.

She thought she heard a mewling sound.

And the little girl inside her who'd never stopped loving animals had to investigate.

She was on her knees in the dirt at the corner of the house when she heard Henry's voice behind her.

"What are you doing?" Clara tensed at Henry's rough question.

Chapter Two

Clara slipped out of the bustling living room and into the farmhouse kitchen, all the way past the wide butcher-block counter. Hiding.

No one had noticed her leave the family gathering, celebrating her great-aunt's birthday. *Aendi* Dorcas.

Clara still wasn't used to the mix of English and German that everyone around her used interchangeably. Living here for two years wasn't the same as growing up in Hickory Harbor.

And that she didn't quite fit in was never more obvious than at a gathering like this.

She'd forgotten about tonight's family event until she'd walked up the quarter-mile gravel driveway and found it packed with buggies and horses. She'd been distracted by thoughts of Henry Barrett's house and the kittens.

Clara had found the mother cat and three day-old kittens beneath the crawl space. The mother had been feral and defensive over the kittens, so tiny they hadn't even had their eyes open yet.

And then Henry had frightened her. He'd been frustrated to see the kittens, but reluctantly agreed with her that they couldn't be moved. The babies were too young.

He might have a gruff manner, but underneath he was kind.

She'd still been thinking about the man when she'd remembered the birthday celebration at home. Only this wasn't her home. It was Great-Aunt Dorcas's house. Clara simply lived here.

Maybe she'd forgotten about the party on purpose.

Even after two years of living with her great-aunt, after joining the Amish church and trying to learn the right ways to live, she still didn't quite fit in.

Great-Aunt Dorcas had a grown son who had daughters only a bit younger than Clara. Emily was twenty and married and Martha was eighteen. Clara thought she was courting and serious about her young man, but Martha and her beau were keeping things quiet and Clara had never been invited into the inner circle of family to be in the know.

Great-Aunt Dorcas lived alone and seemed to like it that way, but she'd been the only one with space, the only relative who had offered to take Clara in when she'd had nowhere to go.

Voices approached, and Clara moved farther through the kitchen, into the mudroom. Without turning the light on, she promised herself she'd go back out and participate in the party soon.

Just not now.

"Is Brian taking you to the singing next Tuesday?" Emily asked her younger sister.

There was a singing coming up? Clara heard sounds of rustling and a plate tapping down on the counter. She brushed a hand over her face. She'd been invited to one singing—an event for the young people to be together and socialize—when she'd first come to Hickory Harbor. And not invited since.

"*Mamm* told me to invite Clara," Martha murmured. "But I don't want to."

The pang of hurt stabbed like a hot iron touching Clara's skin. She pressed her fist against her mouth.

"She's not so bad," Emily said.

"She's so old." Clara heard the words as if Martha had spoken with her nose wrinkled up in disgust.

Twenty-three wasn't that old. Not old enough to be a spinster if one was an *Englisher*. But to Martha, who would probably be married before she was nineteen, maybe Clara seemed an old maid.

"She never talks," Martha complained. Her voice was low, but it carried straight to Clara's heart. "It's so awkward. I never know what to say."

A new flush of mortification washed over Clara. She'd always been shy, always been the quiet one in a room.

"Clara needs a husband," Emily said. "Then *Mamm* might stop asking us to involve her."

Their voices faded away and Clara risked a glance past the doorway. They'd disappeared back into the party in the living room. She was alone again.

But she slumped with her shoulder against the wall. Tears smarted in her eyes and she blinked rapidly to clear them.

Her own cousins thought she was hopeless. Didn't want to be her friends.

Clara needs a husband.

There was also a part of her that was pierced by envy. Emily was younger than Clara was. She was already married and settled and happy. She belonged. She had a place in the community.

If family whispers were to be believed, Emily and her husband were getting ready to start growing their family.

Clara had no one.

At times like this, she missed her mom and dad desperately. Mom had given the best hugs. And Dad would've known what to say to reassure her.

Grandmother and Grandfather hadn't been affectionate. And Great-Aunt Dorcas wasn't, either.

Sometimes the longing for a hug or an affectionate pat on the arm hit so hard that Clara could barely stand it.

Right now she was trembling with missing that kind of touch. That was the only reason she could think of for why Emily's words tumbled and tumbled around in her head.

Clara needs a husband.

She wasn't going to find a husband sitting at home with Great-Aunt Dorcas. And she was so terribly shy that no one dared approach her after Sunday house-church worship.

For one moment, Henry Barrett popped into her head. Henry, with his hair rumpled, crouching on the ground as he took a look at the kittens.

She blinked him away.

She needed an *Amish* husband. One that would help her belong in Hickory Harbor.

But how did she get one?

Henry was late for dinner.

When he walked into the Amish restaurant to meet his brother Todd and his wife, Lena, the place was full.

A young woman in a dress and apron greeted him and when he asked for his brother, she led him to the rear of the crowded restaurant.

Todd and Lena were sitting at a round table meant for six. Todd was turned in his chair and speaking to someone from the next table over.

Lena saw Henry first and her face lit up.

Henry hadn't understood when Todd had first come to Hickory Harbor on a temporary assignment. Todd had been sucked into the fast pace of med school and city life. He was always busy. Until he'd come here.

And when Henry had met Lena, he'd gotten it. She was kind and smart and made his brother laugh.

Falling in love with Lena had also meant his brother had fallen for the slower pace and small-town charm of Hickory Harbor. He'd even joined the Amish church and given up his beloved technology.

And he appeared to be happy here, breaking off from his conversation when Lena nudged him.

"Henry! Hi!" Todd got out of his seat to hug Henry.

He still couldn't get used to his brother's beard. Married Amish men wore them, but Todd had been clean-shaven for as long as Henry remembered.

Another change he didn't quite comprehend.

Henry accepted his brother's embrace and then sat down across the table with his back to the crowded restaurant. It seemed awkward for the three of them to take up such a large table, but Henry brushed it off.

"How was your first day at the house?" Lena asked curiously.

Henry watched his brother settle his arm over the back of Lena's chair. It was a subtle, affectionate gesture, one that showed Todd's feelings about his new wife.

"I didn't get as much done as I expected." He told them about the break-in and the graffiti, about the sheer amount of trash that the previous tenants had left behind.

He couldn't say why, but he didn't mention Clara. She'd popped into his mind as he'd showered at the little motel room a town over that he'd taken. He'd move in to the house when he had one of the bedrooms cleared.

Clara puzzled him.

She'd been painfully shy. Barely whispering words to him.

Until she'd found those kittens. And then she'd been adamant that they not be moved. Eyes flashing, she'd stood in front of that crawl space hole with her hands on her hips and demanded he leave them be.

He'd been so shocked that he couldn't really remember what he'd said.

Something about her taking responsibility for the mother cat and kittens. Which meant he would see her again.

Would she face off with him again?

"The potpie is really good here," Todd offered and Henry realized he'd wandered off in his thoughts.

He'd totally missed the waitress waiting patiently at his elbow and now offered her a smile. He took Todd's advice and ordered the potpie.

When the waitress had gone, he leaned in toward his brother. "How has it been at the clinic? Do you miss the excitement of being in the ER?"

Todd and Lena exchanged an intimate smile that made Henry's stomach knot for some reason. "There's plenty of excitement here," Todd said, turning his attention back to his brother. "I can't give out too many details because of HIPAA laws, but you'll just have to trust me that it's never a dull moment."

Lena waved to somebody across the restaurant.

"I guess everybody in town knows you now," Henry said.

"Everyone is grateful to have Todd. Although it took him a while to come around to our ways." This was said with another smile, one that told a secret only Lena and Todd seem to know.

Henry was beginning to feel like the third wheel. He had bought the fixer-upper because Todd had said over and over that he wanted to rebuild a relationship with Henry.

But maybe it was a lost cause. Todd was married now. He was settled in Hickory Harbor. He had a thriving practice. The differences between him and Henry were as clear as black and white. Would he even have time in his busy life for Henry?

There was movement behind him, and when Todd glanced up and something shifted in his expression, Henry turned to see what it was.

It was David, with Ruby. By his side. Henry's stomach twisted.

Ruby was very pregnant, her belly round under the material of her dress. Her cheeks were a little rounder than when Henry first met her months ago.

"We saw you and thought we would come over and say hello." David said the words to Todd but then his gaze dipped to Henry. There was a slight tension to his posture.

Maybe his tension was Henry's fault. He, unlike Todd, hadn't made an effort to get to know David.

"The girls aren't with you?" Lena asked.

"We wanted an evening to ourselves before this little one comes in a few weeks." Ruby's hand rested tenderly on her stomach.

Henry sat in silence while the flow of conversation moved over him. Todd's brows had crunched and he looked back toward the front of the restaurant. Henry's gaze followed. Past the hostess stand, it had gotten more crowded with people waiting on tables.

"You should join us," Lena suggested.

"Oh." Ruby waved her hand. "We don't want to interrupt your meal together."

Todd started to say something, but it was Lena who gestured to the table. "Our food hasn't arrived yet. And it's late. You're probably hungry."

Henry was seated close enough that he heard David murmur, "You said you were famished."

Meanwhile, Todd looked down at the table. Was his brother looking guilty, or was that Henry's imagination?

He stood up. "I'll be back in a minute."

There was a small vestibule nearby, toward the rear of the restaurant. There were restrooms back here, and an entrance to the kitchen with a swinging door.

Henry stood in the hallway that was out of the flow of restaurant traffic, and away from the dining room. He ran his hand through his hair and then gripped the back of his neck.

"Henry—"

Apparently, Todd had followed him.

Henry turned to snap at his brother. "Did you set this up?"

"No. I didn't."

Henry didn't know whether he could believe his brother.

"Mom called me on the clinic phone."

Todd's words stalled Henry's whirling thoughts.

"She said you've been avoiding her calls. She's worried about you."

Mom had started calling him more frequently about a month ago. She wanted to talk about Nell, Henry's ex-fiancée.

Henry sighed and pushed a hand through his hair. Mom's meddling was bad enough. He didn't need Todd's interference, either.

But there was no mistaking the concern in his brother's eyes.

"What do you want me to tell her if she asks about you again?"

"I'm fine." Henry made his lips curl into a smile to prove it. "I'll call her tomorrow." Maybe.

"You okay if David and Ruby join?"

He wanted to say no.

Henry had grown up without David in his life. The man was a stranger to him. David had been raised by Amish parents after there'd been a hospital nurse that had switched two babies at birth, thirty-something years ago. Eighteen months ago, Todd had done a DNA test and discovered that the infant son their parents had lost couldn't have been biologically related to the Barretts. Todd had started a search for his missing brother that led to Hickory Harbor and David. Todd's discovery had caused a scandal in the sleepy Amish town and changed everything for the Barrett family.

When everything had imploded in Henry's life, Dad and Mom had been distracted by finding David. Their lives had changed for the better.

Henry going off the deep end and missing construction deadlines, almost losing the Dudley house, wasn't David's fault. Logically, Henry knew it was poor timing.

No one in his family knew how bad things had gotten for him.

And that was fine. Working on Dad's Hickory Harbor house was his second chance. He was going to prove himself to Dad and forget about Nell. He was rebuilding.

Henry knew it would be unreasonable to refuse to share a table with David and Ruby. He gave in and forced a smile to his face as they rejoined the table.

David glanced at him with concern and Henry smoothed his expression into a blank mask.

Everything was fine. Or it would be if he could figure out a way to keep Nell from contacting Mom.

He'd been too ashamed to tell his family that Nell had

played him for a fool. She was out of his life and didn't deserve a second chance.

He just needed Mom to leave things alone. But how was he supposed to make that happen?

Chapter Three

Clara stood behind a narrow aisle in the grocery store, not daring to look around its corner. Hiding again.

The store was run by an Amish family and frequented by everyone in their community. Clara had a small bag of cat food in her arms. For the past two days, she had stopped by Henry Barrett's house in the early mornings to feed the mother cat table scraps. The mother cat was still skittish, but what meager food Clara had been able to leave had usually disappeared by the time she returned in the evenings to check on the poor animals.

She needed to make sure the mother was getting the right nutrition for the sake of her tiny kittens.

What she hadn't expected when she had come in was to find a group of young people, all within a few years of her age, standing around the produce section chatting. There was Amos Bontrager, Abel and Sarah Glick, Elsie Meyer and Eli Troyer, who was a bit younger but not much.

"Just go over there and talk to them," she whispered to herself.

But her heart was pounding so loudly that it was drowning out every other sound. Her palms were sweaty, and her chest felt tight, as if she was having a panic attack. She never had one before, but maybe this was what it felt like?

"If you are going to find a husband, you've got to convince someone to come courting. It's not that difficult. Just go over there."

Maybe it was silly to talk to herself like this. On her grandmother and grandfather's farm, she had grown used to having full conversations with the small goats they had raised.

She had been so desperately lonely when she had first come to live with Great-Aunt Dorcas that she had started carrying on conversations with herself.

It was silly, and she was probably far too old for such nonsense, but right now her nerves were getting the better of her and she couldn't help it.

She'd decided that if she had any chance of fitting in, she had to find a husband. But her shyness was so thick it was choking her…

She watched Sarah tip her head in a flirtatious way and tried to imagine herself doing the same thing. She had never had a boyfriend before, never even had a date. Her grandparents had been strict and hadn't wanted her to spend much time with friends, and especially not boys. She had never learned how to flirt. She didn't even know if she could smile like that, the coquettish way that Sarah was. There was an innocence to it. But Sarah was definitely broadcasting her interest in the two young men.

"This is never going to work," Clara whispered to herself. Her shoulders slumped and she turned around, only to realize there was someone standing only a few feet away. Within hearing distance.

Her face flamed as she registered Henry Barrett.

Humiliation crashed over her in a tidal wave.

"Are you giving up so easily?" he asked. His eyes were dancing.

Was he laughing at her?

"How—how long have you been standing there?" she demanded in a tremulous voice.

Henry must have seen how close she was to sudden tears, because his expression cleared of any sign of mirth.

"Hey. I was teasing and—I'm sorry."

Had he overheard everything? She turned her face so she was giving him her profile as she swallowed, attempting to dislodge the lump in her throat.

She'd walked past the group of young people two different times earlier as she'd looked for the cat food. None of them had paid her any attention. She might as well have been invisible.

But not to Henry.

Why did she have to humiliate herself in front of him?

"Great minds must think alike," he said, his voice quiet and even. "I was coming to buy cat food, too."

He was? She'd thought his grudging permission that she could feed the cat meant Henry didn't care about it. But if he was buying food, what did that mean?

He cleared his throat and she thought maybe he was going to excuse himself. She hadn't spoken for over a minute and timidity had her tongue cleaving to the top of her mouth.

But all of a sudden, Henry took a step closer to her. "Thanks to your help, the house was clean enough that I could rip out carpets today." She could only see him in her peripheral vision and caught the grimace as he spoke the words. Why? Because even though they'd carried out enough trash to fill half the dumpster, it still wasn't clean?

"*Onkle* Todd!" A little girl's voice rang out, high and clear, and Clara heard the sound of footsteps tapping on the linoleum floor.

Henry's grimace grew more pronounced and he turned slowly toward the approaching child.

His diverted attention meant that Clara had the chance to back away and escape the embarrassing encounter, but she found her gaze drawn to the little girl.

The girl had stopped short, her eyes wide and prayer *kapp* askew. "You're not *Onkle* Todd," she accused.

"Mindy!" A pregnant woman holding a toddler's hand came around the aisle, moving much slower than the first girl. Mindy. "I told you not to run off." The mother sounded tired.

"I thought I saw *Onkle* Todd." Mindy pouted now.

"You know *Onkle* Todd is working at the clinic," the harried mother said. "Sorry, Henry."

They knew each other? Clara felt the brush of the woman's gaze as she glanced between her and Henry.

"*Onkle* Henry, wouldja buy me a piece of candy?" Pout gone, the little girl now wielded puppy dog eyes.

Onkle Henry?

"Little girls who run off don't get candy," the mother said quickly. "Come along and leave poor Henry to his own business."

Henry wore a thoughtful look as the mother tugged both of the girls away by the hand.

"Is that your...?" Clara let the impertinent question trail off, surprised at herself that it had even emerged from her mouth in the first place.

"It's complicated," Henry muttered. But he was still throwing a look over his shoulder, his eyes narrowed thoughtfully.

"That's for my cat, isn't it?" he asked, nodding toward the bag of cat food in her arms.

"Your cat?" She couldn't say what made the words pop out, instead of a quick agreement.

He half scowled. "You know what I mean. It is? Then, why don't you let me pay for it? We can walk out together."

Why did he want to walk out of the store with her? Her curiosity was piqued, but she also found she'd used up her quota of words and she couldn't just walk out of the store, past the young people, empty-handed.

So she reluctantly let him accompany her to the checkout stand, aware of the curious glances they received. Were the whispers directed at her? She couldn't be sure.

On the sidewalk, Clara clutched the cat food to her middle.

Henry's mind was spinning as he contemplated what had just happened and what to say.

The idea that had occurred to him inside was ridiculous. Maybe too outlandish.

Or maybe it was just outlandish enough to work.

He glanced at Clara, who was holding that small bag of cat food in front of her like it was a shield. She wasn't looking directly at him.

He could still remember the way she'd looked inside. The vulnerability in her eyes, even before they had filled with tears.

He didn't know her. So it didn't make sense that he should care about her feelings. But somehow, he did care.

A crazy idea was rolling around his brain. If he was dating someone new, Mom would have to stop bugging him about Nell. Todd had told him over and over that gossip spread like wildfire in Hickory Harbor. If Henry went on a couple of dates—fake dates—with someone like Clara, word would get back to his brother. He'd already run into Ruby today. It couldn't take long.

And then Todd would tell Mom.

And he wouldn't have to hear about Nell anymore.

He'd been thinking so hard that Clara was looking at him in a way that said she was totally lost.

And she was still holding that cat food. Were her arms tired yet?

"Do you want to put that in your…uh, buggy or something?" He glanced around but saw only one horse and buggy parked nearby. The little grocery store on Main Street didn't have much parking in front of it.

"I walked." Her words were barely audible.

"You did." She'd walked to his job site the other day, too. "Do you walk everywhere?"

This wasn't a big city like Chicago, where a person could walk a few blocks and step on a subway or bus. Hickory Harbor was a small town, but some of the houses and small farms were spread pretty far apart.

Her chin came up. It was the slightest movement, but it was there. "I do."

"Why?"

For a moment, her narrowed eyes made her look like she wanted to refuse an answer.

"I don't have access to a buggy and I can't ride a bike."

He'd seen several Amish teens and even a couple of men riding bikes around town.

"You don't own a bike? Or you don't know how to ride one?"

She sniffed and glanced down the street and he realized they'd gotten offtrack.

"Okay, never mind." He shoved his hands into his pockets. "You want to date an Amish guy, right? Somebody you can eventually marry." That's what he'd overheard her whispering to herself.

Sometime over the past few moments, her blush had faded, but now it bloomed again, casting roses in her cheeks.

Clara started walking down the street. Marching, really.

He followed her, keeping a respectable distance between them.

"If you can't talk to this guy you like—or any guy," he amended when she threw a glare at him, "then how are you going to date him?"

His idea would work. He thought. Maybe.

"What if we pretended to date?" He threw the words out.

Saw her eyes flare wide in surprise before she averted her face. She kept walking.

"Hear me out," he said. It's not like she was arguing with him. "I'm not in town for that long, so it wouldn't be forever. I could help you, you know…"

Henry caught another glare, but he'd already made a fool of himself. Why not keep going? She hadn't said no. Hadn't told him to get lost.

"Learn how to talk to guys."

She stopped walking and whirled on him. "Why me?" she demanded.

It was a good question.

And he ran a sheepish hand through his hair as he answered. "You're the only person I know in town."

It was the wrong answer. He knew it as soon as the words left his mouth.

Whatever tiny spark of interest he'd thought he'd seen in her eyes was extinguished. Her lips pinched and she started walking again.

He followed again, lagging a half step behind this time. "Do you really want to keep doing…that?" He gestured to the store they'd left behind. "Keep hiding behind store displays? Keep wishing for the courage to go up and talk to somebody you like?"

She let go of her burden with one hand and quickly swiped beneath her eye.

Was she crying? Had he upset her that much? His spirits sank.

"Look, I'm sorry," he said. "I didn't mean to hurt your feelings. I thought maybe we could help each other."

He stopped short, letting her outpace him. He turned back the direction they'd come, but just stood there on the sidewalk. He parked one hand on his hip and ran the other one through his hair.

Why was he suddenly so invested in this idea? It had popped into his head when Ruby had looked between him and Clara in the store. He'd noticed her curiosity and how quickly she'd backed away, instead of trying to engage him.

If he was supposedly dating someone, Mom would quit trying to reconnect him with Nell.

Henry sighed.

What he needed to do was go back to the house and get back to work. There were still a couple of hours of daylight left to work.

Stay focused.

Get the job done.

Live up to his responsibilities.

All things his father had taught him. All good things.

But Henry still felt...restless. He wanted to prove himself with this job. Show his father just how capable he was.

He wasn't here to get mixed up in some fake relationship.

What had he been thinking?

Henry started walking back toward his truck.

A prickling awareness on the back of his neck after he'd gone a few steps had him glancing over his shoulder.

Clara had paused just before the next street broke up

the sidewalk. She was still holding on to that cat food. And looking at him.

He stopped. If she wasn't walking away, did that mean she was considering his offer?

Clara didn't come any closer. Henry didn't move.

The autumn breeze blew her skirts against her legs.

For a moment, it bugged him. What was she going to do this winter, when she needed to get around? Would she walk through a foot of snow? In blustery, below-zero wind chills?

It shouldn't matter to him.

She shouldn't matter.

But somehow it still bothered him to think about.

She gave a slight wave. A slight flick of her hand. Maybe he'd even imagined it.

And then she turned and walked on.

What did it mean? *Goodbye*? *Thanks for the ridiculous offer*? *I'll do it*?

He was left standing on the sidewalk, watching her become smaller and smaller until she turned down a side street and then disappeared.

At least he could be fairly sure she wouldn't tell anyone else about his silly idea. She didn't seem to talk to anyone.

And he could live down his humiliation in private.

Chapter Four

Clara trudged along the side of the road toward home. It was misting, and must have been for some time. The temperature hovered near freezing. She could tell, because the blades of grass beneath her feet were slick.

The cold, wet conditions meant the exposed skin of her face and neck was chilled and her skirt was sodden where it brushed the tall autumn grasses.

She disliked this weather. It made her grumpy.

Or maybe her hunger was coloring her feelings.

She should've stayed at the Griegers' home. Dorcas had been feeling under the weather today and had stayed home from house church. Usually, Clara sat next to her great-aunt on the women's side of the room. Worship was one of the only times she felt as if she truly belonged to the community around her. Even when the congregation sang old hymns in German and she didn't know the words or what they were saying, she could close her eyes and let the music lift around her and still feel a part of something.

It was when services ended and the time for socializing began that she felt overwhelmed and set apart.

Clara's right foot slipped and she wobbled on her feet before she was able to steady herself. She took a deep breath and attempted to slow her heartbeat. She could hear a vehicle approaching from a far distance and edged farther away from the road. She didn't know if the pavement was slick and dangerous.

The landscape around her was so quiet. No one was out and about.

Because she'd left the fellowship early.

The noise of the approaching car got louder and she glanced over her shoulder, wanting to determine whether she should move farther from the road, though a muddy ditch would mean risking a slip.

She recognized that truck. It belonged to Henry Barrett.

She quickly turned her face to the front again. She wished her wool coat was a parka, with a big, fur-lined hood that might hide her face. Or that the ground would open up around her and she could just disappear.

Don't notice me.

Drive past.

But Clara's hopes were in vain.

The engine noise of his truck grew louder and then steady as he pulled even with her.

She kept an even pace, though her face flared with heat.

What if we pretended to date?

She hadn't been able to stop thinking about his suggestion since she'd seen him at the grocery store nearly a week ago. *You're the only person in town I know.*

Humiliation scalded her cheeks hotter.

Henry must have felt sorry for her. He'd seen her awkwardness, heard her talking to herself and made her an offer out of pity.

She'd sort of hoped she would never see him again.

It was a silly hope, in a town as small at Hickory Harbor.

The passenger side window of his truck rolled down. "What are you doing out here?"

Walking. She was walking, and it was obvious, and she wasn't going to answer him.

"It's freezing out," he called. "Where are you going?"

He wasn't going to leave her alone, was he?

She gritted her teeth. "I'm fine. I'm on my way home."

She glanced at him only to see him looking pointedly around. There were only two farmhouses in sight, and neither of them belonged to her great-aunt.

"How much farther is it?" he asked.

It wasn't his business, but somehow she knew that he wasn't going to let it go.

Especially when he prompted, "Clara."

"Not far. A couple of miles."

It was awful timing, and she would've prevented it if she could but a shiver wracked her at that moment.

And he saw.

"A couple of miles?" He sounded incredulous.

She didn't mind the walking, usually. She liked having time to think.

But it was cold today.

"I'm used to walking."

It was true, but the bite of cold this morning caught in her lungs with every breath.

Dorcas had wanted to stay home and rest and had insisted Clara attend house church on her own this morning.

When Clara had protested, Dorcas had been adamant. She'd probably hoped her absence meant Clara would have lunch surrounded by new friends, one of whom would be a young man who offered to take her home in his buggy.

But all Clara could think about was the chapter in *Pride and Prejudice* where Mrs. Bennet sent Jane off to the Bingleys' home in the rain.

Only it wasn't an Amish hero riding to her rescue, was it?

"I'll give you a ride home. It'll take at least another hour if you walk."

She tried not to count the time, but he was right. And with her fingers and the tip of her nose going numb, she wanted to accept.

Clara barely knew him. They'd worked together inside his fixer-upper, all day. She knew he was a hard worker.

And she knew his brother, Todd Barrett, affectionately known in town as Doc. The local doctor had a reputation of being trustworthy and compassionate. His brother should be safe.

And she really didn't want to walk in the chilly, misty cold for another hour.

"Thank you," she murmured as he stopped the truck and she crossed the shoulder to meet it.

She pretended not to notice how he turned the heater up as she got in. She was immediately grateful for the warmth inside the cab as she fastened her seat belt.

Silence descended until he spoke.

"This isn't against the rules, is it?"

He must've registered her flare of embarrassed confusion. "For you to ride in a car with me? My brother gave up his car—his pride and joy—when he joined the Amish church."

Oh. "Our church doesn't allow us to own an automobile, but there's no rule against riding in one. For long trips, it's necessary to rent a car and driver or ride on a bus."

The feeling was beginning to return to her half-frozen fingers, and he must've noticed her rubbing them together, because he tilted one of the air vents from his side of the truck toward her.

There'd been no traffic and Henry eased his truck into Drive and took off at a slow pace.

"You don't have a buggy?" he asked.

She shook her head. Technically, the buggy belonged to Dorcas, but Clara was a nervous driver and the horse didn't like her.

"What about a bike? I've seen a lot of Amish riding bikes. It's quicker than walking."

She shook her head.

He glanced at her and she saw his grip on the steering wheel tighten. "You don't like bikes? Can't afford one? Afraid of getting your skirt caught in the pedal?"

She couldn't understand why he was pushing. Dorcas was the only one who spoke to Clara like that and it was usually her impatience driving it. Clara sensed Henry was asking questions out of curiosity.

Why did he care?

The uncertainty made her cheeks hot and she looked down at her lap as she spoke quietly. "I never learned to ride a bike."

She didn't look up, but she felt his glance anyway, like he'd physically touched the back of her hand where it rested in her lap. She resisted the urge to flex her hands.

He wasn't finished asking questions.

"Are you scared of me?"

Henry figured Clara had a right to be nervous around him after the unconventional suggestion he'd launched at her the last time they'd been together.

But there was a part of him that was relieved when she shook her head.

What was her deal? Was she just incredibly shy? She'd spoken to him a few times on the day they'd worked together, but only about work.

He'd seen her hiding in the grocery store.

And today she could barely talk to him. Curiosity nudged

him. What kind of person was this shy? Had she always been like this?

He felt a little sorry for her, walking such a long distance in the unseasonable cold snap. He'd seen on the weather channel earlier today that forecasters were calling for it to warm back up to milder temperatures. Warmer temperatures would be better for the outdoor work at the house that needed to be done.

He was going to just let the conversation die, but she asked, "Can we stop and check on the kittens?"

"Sure." He'd had to drive to the next bigger town to find a lumber store open on a Sunday. The bed of his truck was filled with boards to replace some water-damaged flooring he'd uncovered in the back bedroom when he'd ripped up the carpet.

"Do you live with your parents?" He figured she did. In a town with old-fashioned values like this one, he imagined that's what girls her age did. "Are they gonna mind me dropping you off?"

"I live with my great-aunt."

Oh. He eased off the gas pedal to prepare for the left turn he'd take in a matter of moments.

The silence stretched again.

"You always this talkative?" He didn't know where the words came from, why he'd teased her.

Clara glared at him before she gave him the side of her face.

His phone rang from the center console, and since his phone was connected to the truck via Bluetooth, the caller flashed up on the screen.

Mom.

Henry slowed down, even though there was no oncoming

traffic and no one behind him on the rural road. They were only a couple of blocks from his dad's project.

He hit the button to accept the call, but fumbled the phone and it connected via the truck's speaker system.

"Henry?" His mom's voice rang out in the cab.

Clara's head turned toward him.

"Hi, Mom. I can't—"

"Nell just called me."

Nell. The name body-slammed him and he hit the brakes a little too hard as the driveway approached.

He fumbled for the phone, his suddenly clumsy fingers unable to mash the button so the call wasn't broadcast through his truck anymore.

"She said you won't take her calls. You were engaged for a year and a half—"

He finally got the call disconnected and held the phone up to his ear. Tried to pretend his hands weren't shaking.

"—and she said you blocked her number."

"I know how long we were engaged," he muttered.

In his mad scramble to take the phone call, he'd stopped the truck in the middle of the road, not far from the property's driveway. Now he eased forward, turning into the gravel drive, and put the car in Park.

His face had gone hot, but little trickles of cold slipped down from his scalp and down the back of his neck.

"Do you even know what she needs?" Mom pressed.

He was clenching his jaw so hard he could feel a muscle in his cheek jumping. Nell didn't need him. She'd made that clear when she'd shouted it at him in the middle of a fight, when he'd been doing everything he could to keep the Dudley job from failing, when Dad's health had been in danger.

Clara popped the passenger door open and slipped from the truck. She closed the door softly and he felt a beat of thankfulness for the privacy—and then caught her concerned glance she threw over her shoulder as she walked toward the house.

Great. Now a virtual stranger knew his private business.

"Henry—"

"Mom, I need you to stay out of it." He said the words evenly. Mom and Dad knew about the breakup, but not everything that had happened between Henry and Nell.

"Can't you just take her call? Blocking her seems cruel. That's not like you."

He fisted his fingers and pressed one knuckle into his eye socket. It didn't help. "I have taken her calls."

And blocking her number had only worked for a short time. She'd borrowed a friend's phone or bought a new one, and started calling him from a new number.

"Things are over between us."

Nell had broken his trust. He'd spoken to his pastor about it more than once. He forgave her. But he couldn't be in a relationship with her again. Marriage was completely off the table.

"Mom, please don't speak to her again. What was between us is over and it's my business. Not something she should be trying to talk to you about."

In a way, he was thankful that things had ended the way they had. Henry hadn't known until after how manipulative his ex could be. Like this. Getting his mother involved just so he would take her calls.

"But—"

"Please, Mom." She must've heard the desperate tone in his voice.

"I wish you had someone special in your life."

I do. For one wild moment, he wished he could tell her

he was dating Clara. It would take the pressure off. Prove to Mom that he was over Nell.

But Clara had given him a clear no.

He rang off with his mom and got out of the truck.

Clara was crouching near the hole in the crawl space that he hadn't been able to patch yet. He'd come out a couple of times, trying to convince the mother cat that she'd be better off living in a box, not under his house. It hadn't worked.

He exhaled noisily, trying to release some of the tension from that phone call. He stuck his hands in his pockets and walked over.

Clara had somehow convinced the mama cat to emerge from her hiding place. She was twining in a circle against Clara's knee. Clara was petting her.

The moment he neared, Mama Cat scurried back inside her safe place. He heard tiny mews.

"How'd you do that?" he asked.

Clara shrugged, standing up and brushing her hand on her skirt.

"Do you think she's hungry? The food is in a bin just inside the front door." He hadn't wanted to leave it outside to attract other critters.

"She seems fine for now."

Clara went silent and he let himself look out over some farmer's field across the road. The mist was still coming down, and he didn't want to stand here for long but it was pretty.

Silence descended, but in the aftermath of Mom's call and his bruised emotions, it was welcome.

There was something peaceful about being with Clara. Someone who didn't want anything from him.

Until she said, "You were engaged?"

The muscles in his shoulders went tense again.

He nodded.

He tried to brace for follow-up questions.

But she surprised him when she kept staring across at the field. "What if I reconsidered your offer and you gave me..." She bit her lip, then blurted, "Dating lessons?"

Chapter Five

Dating lessons.

Two days had passed since Clara had made the outlandish suggestion and she still couldn't quite believe she'd done it.

Or help but wonder whether it had been a mistake.

It was early evening and she waited on a wooden bench outside the Amish restaurant in town where she had agreed to meet Henry for dinner.

He was late.

Or was he having second thoughts about doing this with her?

Henry had been the one to suggest they fake a dating relationship in the first place.

Clara's nerves were jangling and it didn't help that everyone who walked past her seemed to glance at her curiously. She felt the weight of their glances each time.

Part of her wanted to disappear. She didn't like the attention.

And part of her wanted to stand up and ask, "What are you looking at?" She was only sitting on a bench, after all.

She hated this.

Maybe Henry had stood her up. Maybe he wasn't coming after all.

Clara saw a tall figure approach from the sidewalk, where

the parking area behind the restaurant funneled out onto the street.

Henry?

No, the man was dressed Amish, in dark pants and a blue shirt beneath his suspenders. Another man joined him, this one younger. Both of them were clean-shaven. Unmarried.

Her heart leaped when she registered Abe Ellis and his younger brother Micah. Her ears started buzzing. What if he spoke to her? He was heading straight for the restaurant.

The brothers were speaking to each other. She saw their mouths moving, but the pulse drumming in her ears drowned out any chance of hearing their words.

Closer. They were almost upon her, would have to pass her to reach the restaurant door.

Abe's eyes began to travel in her direction and she darted her eyes to the ground, afraid to be caught staring.

Another thought chased that one. What if he was looking for an opening to say hello?

Torn, she glanced back up. Only to find his attention riveted on his brother, who was gesticulating with his hands.

Closer.

And then the two young men walked past Clara on her bench, without so much as a glance or a word.

They had completely ignored her. As if she was invisible.

Clara flashed both hot and cold as the noise of the restaurant spilled outside momentarily, then was cut off again as the door shut behind the brothers.

Her stomach pinched.

This entire thing was supposed to help her catch Abe's attention—

She stood up, intending to start the long walk home.

And that's when Henry strode around the corner from the parking lot in back.

Her heart still hurt from the slight of being ignored, but it sped up when she registered the stubble darkening Henry's jaw and how his damp hair curled around the ends.

Unlike Abe, Henry's gaze locked on her immediately. She could still go. If she went inside that restaurant, Abe and Micah would be inside somewhere.

"Hey," he greeted her.

She'd spent all morning cleaning a massive two-story home. The owner hired her once a week and had even given her a key. She never saw a soul. That was the only reason she could give that Henry's simple greeting hit her so hard.

She didn't want him to see, so she dropped her gaze.

"You all right? Sorry I was late. Lost track of time and was running a step behind all day."

She should call this off. Right now. Just excuse herself and walk past him and go home.

But the words were caught in the knot behind her sternum.

Henry sighed. Was he regretting this, too?

He stood at an awkward distance. Not close, like a friend would. Not how she imagined a date would be.

And then before she was really ready for it, he closed the distance between them. Shepherded her toward the door with a hand at her back. Clara could feel the heat coming off of him, his body taller and broader than she was, without turning around. She felt the strange awareness of him at the back of her cheeks, pulsing in the lobes of her ears.

He pulled the door open for her, kept his hand at her back as she preceded him in.

It was too late to call it off now. They'd walked through the door.

Lovina Fisher, whose family owned the place, led them

through the restaurant. It was a weeknight and only half of the tables were full, but Clara felt overly conspicuous.

She was glad to slip into a booth. The back and sides of the booth weren't tall, but at least they offered some privacy.

She couldn't help noticing that Abe and Micah were seated at the back of the restaurant, in a far corner. Abe had his back to her. All this trouble, and he wouldn't even notice.

And then Henry sat down and for a moment he was all she could see.

Lovina took their drink orders and left them with menus.

Clara toyed with hers where it hung over the edge of the table. Henry watched her, not even pretending to glance at his menu.

"You have a busy day?" he asked.

She nodded. It was always a challenge to finish the two-story, five-bedroom house by 5:00 p.m.—the time the owners had requested she be out of the house. With four bathrooms and a massive kitchen, Clara's hands were scrubbed raw. Her back ached from dusting so many knick-knacks and all those rooms of fancy trim.

"You mad at me?"

Her gaze flicked to his face. She wanted to quail under the intensity of his stare.

"Why would I be mad?" She barely spoke above a whisper. "I didn't think you were coming."

Something shifted in his eyes. "I'm sorry."

"You already said that." It hadn't helped the first time. Her skin felt raw, as if she'd doused herself in a bleach cleaning solution.

"Maybe this was a mistake." This time, her words were a whisper.

Something shifted in his expression.

"Can we start over?" he asked.

From the back of the restaurant, she caught Abe peering around the restaurant. He didn't seem to see her, but she was reminded of the whole reason she'd suggested dating lessons. She wanted to marry an Amish husband. Maybe Abe.

And she couldn't marry him if he didn't know she existed.

She hadn't thought the experience would be this painful. But it would all be worth it in the end. Wouldn't it?

"All right. We can start over."

A flash of relief crossed his face.

A different waitress in a prayer *kapp* and lavender dress came to their table—a young woman Clara had seen in church but never met. Her name tag read Eloise.

Clara didn't miss the flash of surprise in her eyes when she took in Clara and Henry together.

Eloise took their orders with a smile, but shot a look over her shoulder as she left the table.

Clara's chest felt hot. This was what she wanted, wasn't it? For the young people her age to know that she was dating material?

"Did you work today?" Henry asked, drawing her attention back to him and out of her whirling thoughts.

"Yes." But he didn't want to hear about her cleaning toilets or scrubbing baseboards. She traced one finger along the edge of the table. "Like any other day."

She swallowed. The conversation stalled. Was it her turn to ask a question? She wished she knew what was supposed to happen.

Henry watched Clara. Her face was so expressive. Did she know she telegraphed every emotion?

She had every right to be irritated. He had lost track of time on the job site. He'd found some water damage in one of the bedrooms that shared a wall with the bathroom and been forced to tear out the drywall there to determine where the water came from.

When he'd looked at his watch late in the afternoon, he'd realized he couldn't show up to dinner covered in drywall dust. He'd taken the world's quickest shower, but he'd still been late.

Clara was too nervous.

He needed to find a conversational route that would help her open up.

He sipped his lemonade. "Tell me about you. Have you always lived with your great-aunt?"

She twisted her water glass on the table. "No. I lived with my paternal grandparents, but they passed away."

Clara glanced up at him and then back at her hands. She must've seen the follow-up question on his face. "My parents died when I was very young."

The words were delivered in a matter-of-fact manner, as if Clara was used to saying them. But he still caught the tremble in her hand.

His stomach twisted. Clara's parents had died, and then the grandparents who'd raised her? He wanted to reach across the table and take her hand, offer her at least that much comfort. But he held back. They barely knew each other.

She drew a trembling breath and Henry blurted, "I'm so sorry."

It didn't help. She was pressing her lips together and blinking rapidly, like she was about to cry.

"Maybe tonight is not my night."

She peered at him.

"I was late and made you anxious," he recounted. "And now I've managed to almost make you cry. I knew I was rusty on the dating front, but I didn't think it would be this bad."

She narrowed her eyes slightly at him, but least she seemed to have backed off from the edge of crying.

"Maybe starting over wasn't the right answer for tonight. Maybe we just need to get all the awkwardness out of the way."

Her eyes went wide, panicked.

Putting one elbow on the table, Henry leaned forward. "Hear me out. I've been embarrassed since Sunday when you heard my phone conversation with my mom."

Even saying the words, he felt heat blooming under his collar.

"This," he waved between them, "isn't a real relationship, so maybe it doesn't matter if you know all the uncomfortable details."

The waitress approached with their meals in hand and he sat back so she could put it on the table. She left with a smile. He'd noticed Clara's preoccupation with the waitress earlier, but this time she barely looked at the girl. Her attention was riveted on Henry.

"Nell and I were engaged. And now we're not."

She had picked up her fork and now it dangled from her hand as she leaned forward on her elbow. "Those aren't details."

He smiled wryly. "You noticed that, huh?"

Henry sighed, and it wasn't an exaggeration. "I thought we were happy, but Nell kept stalling about setting a date for the wedding. I thought she'd decide when she was ready. Instead, she decided to see another guy on the side."

Clara blinked at him. Her expression was one of disbelief, and maybe they didn't know each other at all, but he felt vindicated. A little. He had been blindsided, unable to believe Nell would cheat.

"We broke up." He'd told everyone it was mutual. If that meant that Nell had begged and pleaded for another chance. He might've given her one if he hadn't stumbled upon an email she'd left open on a browser window on his computer.

"And she seemed fine with it for a while. But recently she started blowing up my phone. Now she's apparently calling my mom, who doesn't know about Nell cheating on me."

She took a bite, considering him. "Did you call her? Nell? After your mom phoned on Sunday?"

Henry shook his head. He hadn't had the fortitude to do it. The last voice mail Nell had left him had asked him to meet for coffee. He just couldn't do it. She'd broken his heart and because of the emotional turmoil, he'd failed his dad. It'd taken him a long time to piece himself back together. He couldn't afford to let Nell mess him up again.

Henry wasn't up for more of her emotional games.

"It sounds like a soap opera," she said after chewing and swallowing another bite.

His brow wrinkled. "How do you know what a soap opera is?"

When Todd had told him everything he was giving up to join the Amish church, Henry couldn't believe it. Maybe his brother didn't watch much TV, but for Todd to give up his phone? His car?

"My mother left the Amish church before I was born. My grandparents that raised me were as strict as some Amish parents, but they didn't follow the teaching of the Amish church. They had a TV and my grandmother loved her soaps. When I was ten, she started letting me watch them with her."

Her eyes had gone far off and she looked a little sad. "Were you close?"

She bit her lip and tipped her head down. "Not really."

"Are you close with Dorcas? Is that why you moved here?"

He'd thought she couldn't hide her emotions, but he was wrong. He watched as Clara's face went carefully blank. "When my grandparents died, the bank repossessed their land. I was nineteen with no work experience, no money. I had nowhere else to go."

There was more behind it. Henry could tell by the way she'd cut off her words. There was more she wasn't saying.

"So why'd you stay? Why join the Amish church?"

Todd had, which was still unfathomable to Henry. Maybe if he understood why Clara had done it, he could understand his brother's decision.

She stared at her plate. "On the first Sunday I attended house church with my great-aunt, there was a family whose home had burned down. The entire thing was gone. Down to the foundation. The church, this community, rallied around them. Built them a new home in less than a week. Provided everything they needed to start over. It was what a true church should be. A family."

And Clara wanted that. She didn't have to say it for him to hear it.

She patted her mouth with her napkin, caught him staring. "What?"

Henry shook his head. He couldn't put it into words.

He'd imagined this would be easy. Hang out with Clara a few times, make everyone believe they were an item. It would help them both.

When she'd asked him for dating lessons, he'd thought it didn't change anything.

But it had only hit him just now that Clara was a real

person. Not a caricature, not an actor. She had a past with real hurts in it.

Clara wanted to belong. That's why she wanted to get married. He'd thought it was silly before, or part of the Amish culture. But it was deeper than that.

He cleared his throat when she kept staring at him. She'd gone deep with him, revealed herself. It was Henry's turn.

"I get that. Wanting to have that sense of family. That's why I am rebuilding this house for my dad. To finally make things right."

Clara didn't need a fake date. She needed a friend.

All of today's awkwardness was because he'd gone into this thinking about how they could pretend.

Henry would've done it all differently if he'd known.

They'd made an agreement. He wasn't going to back out on her now. Not when he knew what she'd been through.

He'd start by being her friend, from this moment on.

Chapter Six

Henry was early for his next dating lesson with Clara.

He'd seen her walking past his job site Saturday afternoon and jogged outside to invite her.

It was late afternoon now and he'd picked her up—early!—from the office where she'd been working today.

Clara had been quiet on the short ride here, but now that he'd begun to get to know her better, he didn't mind.

She stared out the passenger window as he pulled the truck into a parking area at the local nature park. The weather had straightened itself out and warm autumn sunshine beamed down, giving gold edges to the red, yellow and orange leaves showing off their colors all around.

Henry took in the smooth paved pathways leading off the parking lot. Perfect.

"What are we doing here?" Clara must've been lost in her thoughts because she roused, looking around.

This late in the day, there were only two other cars in the lot. No Amish buggies.

"Lesson two," he said.

He'd been thinking about this for days. About Clara, if he was honest with himself, through the repetitive work of laying small tiles in the hall bathroom at Dad's job site.

Henry couldn't stop thinking about the sadness in her eyes when she'd told him she wanted to belong here.

And he also couldn't stop worrying about Clara walking everywhere in town. It'd been chilly this morning and the office she worked at today had been far enough away that he knew she'd been on the road before it had gotten light outside. She needed a better method of transportation.

He was going to solve two problems today.

"C'mon." He opened his door and tipped his head, inviting her to join him in the outdoors.

He was gratified when she got out of the truck, albeit a tad reluctantly. They met at the back of his truck, where he reached up to let down the tailgate.

"It's beautiful out, huh?" he asked when he caught her staring at a massive maple throwing shade on the edge of the paved parking area. This was the kind of weather he loved. Perfect for grabbing a friend for an impromptu hiking trip, though he hadn't done that in a while. Or catching a pick-up football game with some of the guys from church. It'd been too long since he'd joined in.

Now wasn't the time to focus on how busy Henry had been.

Clara had wrapped her arms around her middle, glancing around. Was she nervous?

"What are we doing here?" she asked. "How will anyone see us?"

She meant *what was the point*, even if she was too polite to say so. This wasn't the Amish restaurant or someplace in town where they'd be seen and her future beau would finally notice her.

"Today, we're going back to basics. We need to work on your confidence." He'd been thinking about this nonstop and even gone so far as to do an internet search for dating tips—that one had gotten him out in the weeds.

Her lips pinched together.

Henry rushed on, in hopes of not offending her. "Check it out." He threw back the tarp that had been covered his surprise in the truck bed.

A bike.

The confusion on her face grew.

"It's not new." Henry moved around the side of the truck to tip the bike upright, then pushed it toward the end of the truck bed so he could lift it onto the ground.

Clara actually backed up a step.

"What do you think? I found it at a garage sale in Apple Bend." He'd visited the next small town over last Saturday to pick up a fixture for the bathroom sink and had circled the block twice before stopping at the curb to ask about the bicycle.

It was a unisex bike, a cruiser-style and not a mountain bike. Made for neighborhood riding. It was sturdy and he'd checked the brakes and aired up the tires before he'd put it in the truck today.

"It's not for me." Clara said the words not quite like a question but not like a statement, either.

"Sure it is."

She shook her head, her eyes wide. "I told you I don't know how to ride a bike."

"I know. But you can't keep walking everywhere once it gets to winter."

What happened when the weather was below freezing?

"Plus, think about the confidence you'll gain when you learn a new skill," he said.

"This isn't actually a dating lesson at all." Clara had a stubborn set to her mouth, now looking off to the side.

Obviously, Henry hadn't explained this well at all.

"Confidence is important," he said. "There's something about a girl who knows who she is that's attractive."

A memory of Nell and the way she'd used to toss her hair over one shoulder when they'd met at a singles event at church flashed through his brain.

Clara was listening to him, her eyes flicking to the bike, to him, and then back to the bike.

"I won't let you get hurt, if that's what you're worried about." He could remember his dad teaching him to ride when he'd been about seven. Henry had never taught anyone himself, but it couldn't be that difficult, could it?

Clara still looked uncertain. "I thought you were bringing me to see the kittens."

He smiled. "I'll take you by the site when we're finished here. Their eyes are open today."

She pulled a face. "Fine."

"You'll do it?"

"Okay."

He pumped his fist in the air, but she glared at him. "I don't think it will work. Riding a bike won't make me more interesting to—" She cut herself off. Henry didn't understand why. What would it hurt if he knew the name of the guy she liked?

He shrugged that thought off.

"Let's find a footpath surrounded by some grass—just in case." He began wheeling the bike off the asphalt parking area to where one of the paths led farther into the park.

"How does it work?" she asked, trailing him. "I mean, I know the mechanics."

"You've never ridden at all. Never tried?"

She shook her head. "After my parents died, I lived on

my grandparents' small farm. There was no pavement. Nowhere to ride."

He and Todd had ridden everywhere together—even places not meant for bikes.

"But what about—did you never see anyone riding their bike to school? Feel curious, want to try it?"

"I was schooled at home. We didn't go to town much. I didn't have many friends."

Another piece of the puzzle that was Clara clicked into place. She'd been raised by two grandparents who kept her isolated. Homeschooled. No friends.

No wonder she was shy. She just didn't know how to approach getting to know someone new.

This was going to work. Henry felt it.

This was going to be a disaster.

Clara wasn't afraid—not exactly. She just didn't want to humiliate herself in front of Henry.

That wasn't prideful, was it? Maybe. She sent a prayer heavenward for repentance.

"Here," Henry said.

He hadn't seemed to notice her discomfort. Or maybe it didn't bother him.

He had been pushing the bike by its handlebars and now he stepped back slightly, only holding on to one side.

Motioning toward the seat, Henry raised his eyebrows expectantly.

Clara swallowed hard. Glanced around.

There was a mother putting her two young children into a minivan and one other vehicle in the parking lot, besides Henry's. There was no one to see her make a fool of herself.

She took hold of the handlebars, but the bike wobbled when Henry let go. He gripped his side again.

"How am I supposed to keep from falling?" She hated that her voice trembled.

"It's all about momentum," he said. "The faster you go, the easier it is to balance."

"I don't want to go fast."

He raised one expressive eyebrow at her. Possibly because of how quickly she'd said it.

"We'll only go as fast as you want. Why don't you just try getting on it?"

Clara didn't want to.

But she sighed and put one leg over the middle bars, standing so she straddled the bike.

"Good. Can you sit on the seat?"

It was awkward and this time she wobbled so mightily that Henry moved to stand in front of the bike so he could hold both handlebars steady. Which also meant she had to look at him head-on.

He was handsome.

She'd had the realization sitting across from him in the restaurant. With his blue eyes framed with sinfully long lashes and the streaks of gold hidden in his dark hair, he reminded her of one of the TV stars from a show her Gram used to watch.

It felt too difficult to meet his intense gaze directly.

"Now what?"

"Can you sit on the seat? Try putting one foot on the pedal," he added when she'd done the first.

It felt unsettling with Clara's weight on the seat. Only one foot propped her up, and Henry was steadying the handlebars.

"Think you can take your other foot off the ground?"

She shook her head. Her hands felt shaky, sweaty on the rubber grips.

"Clara." He waited until she was clearly listening. "I won't let you fall. Promise."

"You can't promise that." She sounded a little breathless. Felt that way, too.

Henry's fingers brushed her right hand, though he hadn't moved his grip on the bike, still holding it steady.

Startled, her gaze flew up to clash with his.

"I promise."

Henry's stare was probably meant to be reassuring, but it was the steady confidence deeper in his gaze that drew her. What must it be like to feel that?

She gulped a deep breath. "Okay."

But she could only lift her foot an inch off the ground. What if she fell?

His lips tipped in a sideways grin. "You'll have to get your foot all the way on the pedal."

Clara didn't know if she could. What if the bike fell over?

"Hang on."

She rested her foot back on the ground as Henry took a few steps that brought him next to her instead of in front of the bike. He held the handlebar, and with his hand right next to Clara's, she registered how broad his was compared to hers. *He* was broad. And she could feel the warmth coming off of his body.

"Ready?"

She grimaced at his question but brought both feet to the pedals. True to his word, he didn't let her wobble.

Clara's heart was flying in her chest as he slowly pushed her forward.

"We'll be riding along together before you know it." She couldn't take her eyes from the path in front of her, but she heard the smile in his voice.

"You ride?"

"Since I was a boy. My brother taught me." His voice deepened with some emotion. Clara sensed more than saw him shake his head.

When silence lengthened, her nerves began to jangle. She gripped the handlebars tighter.

"Tell me about when you learned. Did you fall?"

Henry kept pushing at a steady, slow pace. Weren't his arms getting tired? He showed no sign of it.

"I don't remember falling—then. I remember being too short to reach the pedals. Standing on this curb out in front of our house so I could get on the bike. Turning around in a neighbor's drive because it was big and wide.

"I do remember a bad fall. I was showing off for a girl— riding with no hands."

Somehow while Henry was speaking, she'd relaxed.

She tried pushing the pedals through one rotation. That wasn't too bad.

"Do you want to stop?" she asked. "I'm probably too heavy to keep pushing."

"No, you're not. I could keep going like this all evening long."

Clara felt a slow blush heat her neck and seep up to her cheeks. "You'd do that?"

"Yeah. I want you to succeed." That quiet confidence was back. This time directed at her.

Henry was starting to feel like a true friend.

"I—I think I could try. By myself."

He let her roll to a stop, took a step back as she put her feet down and stood over the bike on shaky legs.

His brows were raised as he watched her. "You sure?"

"Sort of."

Clara took a deep breath and pushed against the pedals. The bike moved forward and she wasn't ready—

The wheel wiggled back and forth on the pavement—
She overbalanced and tumbled—
Clara crashed to the ground, the bike on top of her legs.

Her right hand throbbed where she'd landed on it. Tears pricked her eyes as Henry rushed to her side and moved the bike.

He let her roll to a sitting position. She clutched her hand close to her body. The ache was slowly wearing off.

Reaching out, he touched her wrist gently. "Can I see?"

When he gently tugged her arm away from her body, a red scrape was visible on her wrist. Blood oozed slowly from it.

"Maybe that's enough for today."

Chapter Seven

It was Sunday again.

A week from when she'd uttered the words, "dating lessons." And a day after the disastrous bike riding attempt.

Clara sat in the Jonathan Glick family's basement, where two rows of chairs had been pushed to one side of the space for the women, facing the men who occupied two rows of chairs on the opposite side of the room.

She'd been running late this morning after checking in on Great-Aunt Dorcas, who was still complaining of a bad cough, and then feeding the horses. No matter how quickly Clara had walked, the two miles to the Glick's home was too far away to make up the time she'd lost.

If Henry's bike lesson had gone better, she might've been on time.

Last night, she had walked the bike up the driveway after asking Henry to drop her off at the road. She still hadn't brought up their deal to Dorcas and didn't want her great-aunt asking questions. Clara had wheeled the bike all the way behind the barn, so she didn't have to feel the humiliation of falling over and over again.

The last prayer was offered, signaling the end of worship.

Clara stood, along with everyone else.

She'd come in and occupied the only empty seat, next to a young woman about her age, who'd been sitting with her family. Clara wanted to ask whether they were staying for lunch.

But the moment everyone stood up, the young woman turned to speak to the younger sister on her other side, and Clara was given her shoulder.

It wasn't an intentional slight. At least, that's what Clara tried to tell herself.

Clara stretched up on tiptoe, trying to see whether one of her cousins was in the room. She'd rushed inside after the singing had already begun and taken the first, closest seat. She had been too embarrassed to crane her neck during the worship time to see whether Martha or Emily was in attendance. After what she'd overheard before, she didn't want to ask if she could eat lunch with them. But they were family.

Martha was there. She'd crossed the room, along with her mother, to speak to her boyfriend, Samuel, and his family. Martha was glancing around the room idly and her gaze met Clara's.

Clara started to smile and raise her hand to wave, but Samuel said something and Martha turned back to the conversation.

She's so awkward. So old.

Her cousin's words came back to echo in her memory.

Martha hadn't taken a split second to motion Clara over. Or to say something to her beau and then head Clara's direction.

Clara was left alone, standing on the fringes of the entire gathering.

Her stomach pitched and she turned to leave. Two large families blocked the staircase leading to the first floor. The adults stopped to chat while children chased each other through their legs.

Clara was too much of a mouse to speak up and utter a simple, "Excuse me."

She wished the ground would open up and swallow her whole. What was she even doing here?

She was going home.

Stomach grumbling at the thought of skipping the luncheon, Clara hesitated. Or maybe she just felt nauseous at the thought of not a single person in the gathering speaking to her.

"Clara. Hey."

The male voice prompted her heart to beat in her ears and she could feel the heat radiating from her cheeks when she turned to face Henry, who'd approached from the side and slightly behind her.

He looked out of place in his *Englisher* clothes, a pair of dark blue jeans and a patterned button-up shirt, open at the neck and with his sleeves rolled up to show his forearms.

Clara was conscious of the still-healing scrape on her wrist; moments ago she'd been invisible, but now she felt the eyes of numerous people on her. Or was she imagining it?

"What are you doing here?" she murmured, barely resisting the urge to tuck her chin to her chest.

"I came with my brother."

Henry seemed perfectly at ease, perfectly confident as he smiled at her with twinkling eyes. "And then when service ended, I saw you and I thought…why not make time for another lesson?"

He said the words quietly and no one around seemed to be paying attention, but she still felt the tips of her ears go hot.

Todd Barrett approached, his beautiful wife behind him. She'd seen the doctor around town, but up close it was clear he was related to Henry, with the same dark hair, blue eyes and cheekbones.

"Why don't you join us?" Henry asked as Todd and his wife got within hearing distance.

Bad idea.

The words got stuck in her throat and Henry didn't seem to notice her discomfort as he turned to include his brother in the conversation. "You guys don't mind if Clara joins us, do you?"

There was a definite gleam of curiosity in the woman's eyes. The doctor was more reserved. He assessed her with a cool intelligence.

"I'm Todd Barrett," he said. "This is my wife, Lena."

"Oops," Henry said. "This is Clara Templeton. A friend."

The families blocking her exit had moved upstairs to the first floor by now and others were moving to follow.

Henry let Todd and Lena take the lead and when their backs were turned to go up the stairs, Clara sent him a wide-eyed look. What was he doing?

Henry winked at her and it did something funny to her insides. She jumped when he set his hand at her lower back to nudge her up the first step.

She jabbed her elbow into his side, eliciting a muffled grunt.

"What lesson?" she whispered frantically.

Henry glanced ahead, and apparently satisfied that they were out of earshot, leaned in to murmur in her ear, "Widen your circle of acquaintances."

Clara almost missed a step and Henry steadied her.

His touch at her back was gone almost as soon as it came, but Todd had glanced back at just that moment.

She felt self-conscious, especially when Todd's gaze flicked from her to Henry and back. His wife said something and he turned back to face the front as they gained the first floor.

Scents of savory and sweet foods hit Clara's nose and

her stomach twisted with hunger this time. Surely she could make it through one lunch with Henry and his family?

Henry and Clara joined the two lines of people snaking through the kitchen. The afternoon had warmed and the Glick's home was built in such a way that it would be difficult for everyone to sit and have a place to eat inside. Young men traipsed through with chairs from the basement, adding to what was already outside for a modified picnic.

Todd handed Henry a plate, one that he passed to Clara without a thought. She felt a warmth beat inside her, a recognition that he had taken care of her, even in such a minor way.

Lena leaned past Todd as they waited to approach the first long serving table, set out buffet-style with food each family had contributed to the potluck meal. "Where did the two of you meet?"

Clara's thoughts halted. She felt as if a boulder blocked her throat. "Umm…" She glanced to Henry for help.

"We're neighbors," he said easily. "In fact, Clara found the mama cat under my house. She's been helping me take care of the freeloader and her babies."

Lena seemed to accept that, or maybe it was simply her turn to start filling her plate.

Motion across the room caught Clara's attention. There was Abe, entering through the back door. His hands were empty—had he just brought an armload of chairs outside? His younger brother leaned in to whisper to him and Abe's gaze jumped to Clara and then away.

Had he noticed her here, with Henry on one side and Henry's Amish brother and sister-in-law on the other?

Clara felt abruptly cold and then hot. This was what she wanted, wasn't it? Catching Abe's attention?

She could hear decades-old whispers of her grandmother's

criticism. And Clara wasn't entirely sure she could make it through lunch without making a fool of herself.

This wasn't going to work if Clara stayed silent throughout lunch.

Henry was already catching a whiff of suspicion from his brother. Lena seemed curious and interested in meeting Clara, at least.

How could Henry get her to loosen up? Clara was far too nervous. What did she think, his brother was going to give her an anatomy test?

They shuffled forward to a selection of fruit and Jell-O salads and a meat and cheese spread that looked delicious. It probably was.

"You don't like Waldorf salad?" Henry reached for the serving spoon when she passed over the bowl.

Clara wrinkled her nose.

"It reminds me of my grandma." Henry caught Todd's glance and the tic in his brother's cheek. Gramps had gone radio silent after Todd had given up the prestigious ER job at the hospital where his family had been doctors for generations. Todd was happy and settled in Hickory Harbor, but it still had to hurt.

Clara handed Henry a pair of tongs for the last piece of fried chicken on a platter. Their fingers brushed and her gaze jumped to his, then she quickly lowered her eyes.

"You should have it," she said. "It's the last one."

Aha! She'd spoken. He didn't know why it gave him such a sense of triumph, but it did.

Henry picked up the chicken thigh, but put it on her plate instead. "I've been listening to your stomach growl since we ran into each other."

Clara started to protest but he pointed down the serving table. "There's more."

There was another platter, still half-full of chicken. Even if there hadn't been, Henry was going to give her that piece of chicken. Clara needed it more than he did.

"What'd you bring?" he asked as they neared the dessert section.

"Cookies."

"Which ones?"

She pointed to a half-full plate of fluffy chocolate chip cookies and Henry picked one up. He bypassed his plate to take an immediate bite.

The taste flowed over his tongue and he found himself momentarily rendered speechless, only able to groan in appreciation.

Apparently he'd been loud enough to draw Todd's attention. His doctor brother, ever ready to jump into action if something was wrong, was scanning his face for signs of distress.

Henry quickly chewed and swallowed. "You have to get one of these." He took a second one, even if it wasn't polite, and added it to his plate. "Clara made them and they are divine."

Pink dotted Clara's upper cheeks but he definitely caught a hint of pleasure as she ducked her head.

He stuffed the rest of the cookie in his mouth as he followed Todd and Lena to an open patch of chairs. He was so focused on Clara beside him, the swirl of her dark blue skirt and the shy smile she sent his way, that he didn't realize Todd had led them to seats right next to David and his family.

Henry drew up short, shooting Todd a betrayed glare. His brother only looked at him mulishly. Henry couldn't make a scene. He didn't want to ruin his brother's reputation in town. Todd was well respected and should stay that way so people would come to him for medical treatment. And he didn't want to give Mom one more thing to worry about.

Even if that's what Henry wanted to do.

He slipped into the seat on Lena's other side, as far away from David and Ruby as he could manage.

Clara sat beside him. He could feel the concern radiating off of her.

He stuffed a fluffy golden biscuit into his mouth but it tasted like ash.

David had Maggie on one knee and Mindy on the seat between him and his pregnant wife. The girls were chatting more than they were eating.

During a lull in conversation, Mindy asked, "Who's that with *Onkle* Henry?"

Todd cleared his throat pointedly. "Henry, aren't you going to introduce Clara?"

Henry took back every kind thought he'd ever had about his brother.

He made introductions through clenched teeth. Ruby and David were welcoming but there was no missing the curious gazes.

He went back to stewing and eating in silence.

"You don't get along with your brother?" Clara leaned in to whisper the words.

He shrugged. He'd lost his appetite and rested his plate on his knee.

"Do you dislike him?"

Henry wished she wouldn't push.

And then remembered how she'd gotten up from falling off that bike with her hands all scraped up. He could see the edges of her scabbed skin on her wrist, though she was keeping her arm tucked close to her body.

Clara probably had a right to push him.

"I don't know him," he whispered back.

She wrinkled her brow and shook her head slightly in confusion.

"Long-lost brother? Babies switched at birth?"

She still didn't show any sign of knowing what he was talking about. Clara must be the only person in Hickory Harbor who didn't know. Todd had once confessed—though Henry had told him he didn't want to know—that the news had spread through the town like wildfire.

"What are you two whispering about?" Todd asked.

His brother seemed to want to stir up trouble today.

"Clara doesn't know about our family history." Henry said the words to Todd but kept his eyes on Clara. He was speaking plenty loud enough for David and Ruby to hear.

It was Ruby who answered, drawing his attention to her gentle words and demeanor. "That might be something better discussed in a private setting. Why don't the four of you come for supper on Thursday?"

He heard Clara's soft intake of breath, felt the way she'd gone still beside him. An invitation for the four of them made it seem like they were together. Dating. Like their ruse was working.

"I'm busy with the house," he hedged.

Todd gave him a look like he didn't believe him.

It was true, though. Henry had been affixing Sheetrock in the back bedroom until late last night. He was pretty sure he still had gray dust under his fingernails.

His siblings seemed to let it go. Conversation shifted and all he wanted to do was get out of there. Henry had known David and Ruby would be present in house church today. He'd foolishly hoped he wouldn't run in to them.

"Oh!" Next to him, Lena let out an excited gasp. She

nudged Henry's arm. "I just remembered what I wanted to ask you. Hickory Harbor is hosting a volleyball tournament. Todd and I have joined a team—it's coed—but we need more players." She leaned past him to see Clara. "Do you like volleyball?"

Clara looked like a deer in headlights. "I don't know."

"All skill levels are welcome." Lena's words encompassed them both now. "You should think about joining. It'll be a fun time to get to know people." She nudged Henry again. "If you're half as competitive as your brother, you'll want to play."

Todd grumbled playfully from Lena's other side.

When Henry glanced at Clara, she shook her head tightly. He couldn't help smiling. "I didn't say anything."

She pointed her fork at him. "You're thinking it."

"Who else is on your team?" he asked Lena. "Maybe it's someone Clara knows."

"It's two teams, actually. We'll practice together but play separately." She rattled off a list of names.

He watched Clara. Sure enough, she blushed when one of the guy's names left Lena's lips.

Henry bounced his eyebrows at her. "Sounds like we should think about playing."

She narrowed her eyes at him. "I don't know how to play."

"You should both come over to David and Ruby's for dinner. We can bring a volleyball and you can get an idea of what it's like."

He hadn't seen David or Ruby lean over and say anything to Lena, but she seemed just as keen to wrangle him to this impromptu dinner as his older brother. Had his brothers and their wives planned it beforehand?

It left a bad taste in Henry's mouth.

Being around David made him uncomfortable. David's presence reminded him of the weeks-long period when Henry had discovered just how deep Nell's infidelity had run. He'd spiraled and been too absorbed in his perfectly ordered life falling apart and left facets of the Dudley job incomplete. Dad had risked losing his funding from the bank and Henry's mistake could've cost thousands of dollars if Dad hadn't come in at the last minute and saved the project.

Todd cleared his throat, breaking Henry from his thoughts.

Clara glanced uncertainly at him. This sounded like exactly the chance she wanted to get closer to a future beau. Playing a sport was casual and she could build a friendship with whatever Amish guy she picked.

But that didn't mean Henry needed to eat dinner at David's house.

How far was he willing to go to prove to Mom he was okay?

Chapter Eight

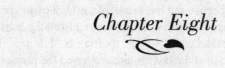

"I'm not sure I'll be any good at this."

Clara looked at the white ball Lena had in her hands as they stood in David and Ruby's wide backyard. Ruby sat in a wooden rocking chair that her husband had moved off the porch and into the grass, in a patch of shade thrown by the house and the afternoon setting sun.

Lena tossed the ball up and caught it. She made it look easy.

"I've never even held a volleyball," Clara added.

Lena tossed her the ball and she reflexively put out her hands, though she missed and the ball whacked her mid-section before she got her hands around it. It hadn't hurt. The ball was lighter than she thought.

"You never played sports? Not even for fun?" Ruby asked.

Clara shook her head. "I wasn't allowed."

Lena frowned. "Were your grandparents strict?"

It wasn't that. Clara tossed the ball to Lena. "It was more that there was never any time. They owned a small farm and keeping it running kept them busy from morning to night."

They'd been too busy for her to join programs like the Girl Scouts or attend youth group events at church regularly. There'd been no sleepovers. Not that she'd had any friends close enough to ask.

"Did you ever play, Ruby?" Lena asked.

The pregnant woman shook her head. She'd seemed a bit quieter tonight than she had been on Sunday. Maybe she was tired. "My *mamm* wouldn't have minded if I had wanted to join a volleyball team." She tipped her head to one side. "My *daed* might've been considered strict, but *Mamm* balanced him out."

Strict. It was a good word to describe Great-Aunt Dorcas. Clara had been too nervous to tell her anything about Henry. She was surprised that one of the cousins hadn't already told that she'd sat with an *Englisher*—and his Amish family—on Sunday at lunch. She knew how Dorcas felt about her mom leaving the Amish church for an *Englisher*. If she knew Clara was friends with Henry, she might be upset.

And Clara felt that Henry's plan was working. She'd caught several glances from young people her age during lunch on Sunday. The longer she'd sat beside Henry and engaged with his family, the easier it got to ignore them.

Maybe, if Abe noticed her, she'd someday have the courage to speak to him.

Sooner rather than later, if Henry had his way.

Thinking of Henry meant her gaze flicked to where she'd last seen him, over near the horse pen outside David's barn. He stood beside Todd, his back to her.

She completely missed the ball Lena tossed in her direction and it flew past her.

"Sorry!" She jogged after the ball, catching a knowing gaze that passed between Lena and Ruby when she had scooped it up and turned back to the women. Her face flamed. "I was distracted."

Lena smiled knowingly. "The Barrett men can be very distracting. Is Henry taking you to the singing next week?"

This question was so nosy that Clara overshot her toss

to Lena. The ball went completely wild, heading in Ruby's general direction.

Ruby got up from the chair, slowly.

"I'll get it," Lena chided kindly. "You rest."

Ruby rubbed at a place low on her belly, her other hand coming to her lower back. She looked a bit pale. "Between David and you and Todd chiming in, I'm resting all the time. I need to stand up and stretch."

A grimace crossed Ruby's features and Clara felt a beat of concern. Lena must've noticed, too, because she detoured from where she'd been walking to get the ball to come to Ruby's side.

Clara sidled a bit closer, still several yards away.

"Should I send Todd to the carriage to get his medical bag?" Lena asked.

Ruby exhaled a burst of air. Her body seemed to relax. "No, no. It's only those Braxton Hicks contractions again. Besides, I want to know about Clara and Henry."

Clara's face flamed hotter but she came when Lena motioned her closer.

"You sure?" Lena asked.

Ruby nodded. "I've been keeping track, like you told me. They come and go."

Lena seemed satisfied with that. Enough that she walked away from Ruby to fetch the ball. And then two curious gazes were turned on Clara.

"I—don't know whether we are attending the singing." She almost winced at her wording. *We.* Like she and Henry were a pair, two of something that belonged together.

She looked away, careful to keep her face averted from where the men stood.

There was a beat of silence and then a soft sigh from Ruby. "I wish I knew how to get David to open up to Henry."

A glance at Ruby's expression showed an echo of hurt. For her husband?

When she caught Clara looking, she smiled a little. "It was hard on Henry," she explained, "when Todd figured out the mystery of two baby boys, switched at birth. I'm sure he's told you about it."

He'd only given her the bare facts, in the car on the way home from house church. She'd felt that he hadn't wanted to tell her, not really, but that he'd had no choice since his family had brought it up.

Now when she looked back at the men, she saw how Henry put slightly more distance between himself and his two brothers than Todd and David had between them. The set of Henry's shoulders was different. Tense.

"Todd has been worried about Henry," Lena chimed in. "Him coming tonight has to be a good sign, doesn't it?"

Clara wasn't so sure. Henry threw a look over his shoulder and his stormy eyes connected with hers briefly.

"I don't suppose you have any house projects?" Clara heard herself say.

When she looked back at the other two women they seemed interested.

"A leaky faucet? Loose floorboard? A new post for your laundry lines? Henry is very good at working with his hands. And if he could feel useful…it might—"

"Make him feel more warmly toward his brother," Lena finished, interrupting. "It's a *wonderbarr* idea. Ruby?"

The other woman wrinkled her nose. "I have been asking David to replace a wobbly shelf under our kitchen cabinets, but he has been helping more with the girls while I'm—" she gestured to her pregnant belly "—and he hasn't had time."

"That's perfect!" Lena crowed.

The men must've somehow registered the excitement in her voice. All three of them turned around.

"Suppertime?" Todd asked.

Lena laughed a little. "He's always hungry."

"I didn't have time to make dessert," Ruby said. "He'll be disappointed."

"I could bake some cookies," Clara heard herself offer. She was blushing fiercely but both women had lit up.

"After supper," Ruby agreed.

Henry was lying on the floor with his head and one shoulder underneath Ruby's kitchen cabinet as he attempted to locate the last hole where he needed to attach a screw. He'd drilled the shelf himself, out in David's father's workshop.

David's adoptive parents lived next door to his house and his father made furniture, so when Ruby had asked Henry during dinner whether he could fix the shelf David hadn't had time for, using the workshop seemed a natural answer.

Except that David had gone with Henry. David had stayed out of his way, only offering help when Henry was clearly stumped by one of the pneumatic saws. David had been helpful and kind. And Henry was finding it hard to hold on to his determination to keep his distance from the man.

It wasn't David's fault that Dad had been disappointed in Henry. Or that he wanted to sell.

Henry was man enough to admit that he was wrong— to himself, anyway.

He could accept David without the two of them being best friends.

There. His index finger brushed over the drilled hole in the wood and he reached for the screwdriver he'd left lying near his thigh.

"Whatcha doin' now?" Mindy's voice was muffled as she spoke to Clara.

There was rustling above him and down at the other end of the counter. The last time he'd looked, before he'd ducked beneath the cabinet, Mindy had been standing on a straight-backed chair pulled up to the counter, while Clara had pulled together ingredients for her delicious cookies.

She'd insisted Ruby rest in the living room and David, Todd and Lena had followed, too. She was left with the little girls and Henry.

"I'm combining the butter and sugar," Clara said. He could hear the rhythmic tap of her spoon against the edge of what must be a mixing bowl.

Something blocked the light coming in from behind him, where he'd opened the next cabinet door over and put all the pots and pans on the counter above him.

A tiny hand patted his shoulder and he startled, jerking hard enough to knock his head against the cabinet door.

"*Onkle* Henwy, ow," said Maggie's tiny voice. He'd been utterly surprised tonight at how many words the two-and-a-half-year-old could say.

He twisted his head to look at her and she patted his cheek. Maggie had somehow crawled her whole body inside the open cabinet and now lay with her cheek propped on one chubby hand.

"Henry? Are you all right?" Clara's stirring had stopped.

His head throbbed where he'd bumped it but he'd had worse. "I'm fine. You're blocking my light, though, stinker." He would've reached up to tweak her nose if he hadn't been concentrating on twisting the last screw in at this awkward angle—he wasn't even sure he could move his arm that direction in this tight space.

"I not a stinker," Maggie said.

"Yes, you are," Mindy muttered from the background.

The light from the battery-powered lamp he'd set on the floor behind him went dim before he heard, "Come here, you silly girl." Somehow Clara said the words with a giggle in her voice and charmed Maggie out of the small space.

"You remind me of your *onkle*'s kitty. She likes to hide in tiny spaces, too."

"She's not my cat," he called out.

Not that Clara or the girls paid him any mind. He heard the scrape of a chair against the floor and Mindy's voice. "What color is she?"

Maggie echoed, "Kitty!"

"Black and orange, with a tiny bit of white on her paw, like she stepped in white paint."

A spoon banged on the counter and he heard Clara's stirring start up again.

"Now we want to add an egg."

"Oh, can I crack it?"

He let their murmurs fade away as the screw slipped into place and he twisted the screwdriver the last few turns, securing it tightly. It took some effort to extricate himself from beneath the cabinet, and then he emerged into the brightly lit kitchen that smelled of sugar and flour.

Clara had Maggie on one side and Mindy on the other. Her hands were covered in flour and she was smiling at Maggie.

He'd been right to bring her tonight. Even though Henry hadn't wanted to come to David's. She'd opened up like a flower in the spring sunlight, chatting easily with Lena and Ruby over dinner, and now this with the girls.

He let his shoulder rest against the closed cabinet door behind him and just watched. She was encouraging to Mindy as the girl stirred whatever was in that bowl—even when Mindy managed to spew flour out of the bowl and onto the counter and floor. When it was Maggie's turn to stir, Clara kept one gentle arm around the tot so she wouldn't topple off the chair as she leaned into the counter.

Clara would be a good mom. She was caring and gentle and didn't seem to mind the twenty bazillion questions the girls kept peppering her with.

At least not until Mindy asked, "Are you *onkle* Henry's girlfriend?"

Clara froze and threw a panicked look over her shoulder.

He took that as his cue to haul himself off the floor. He stepped over to Mindy and lifted her off the chair, setting her on the floor. "None of your business, kid."

Mindy pouted but her eyes were twinkling. He stepped around Clara and lifted Maggie down to the floor, too.

"The sooner you two stinkers let Clara get those cookies in the oven, the sooner we can eat them."

The girls shrieked and ran into the living room, as he'd meant them to do.

"Wash your hands!" Clara called after them. She was already scooping dough into spoonfuls and spacing each dough ball onto a waiting cookie sheet.

"Those two…" he said, shaking his head.

"They are sweet," she argued gently.

"They're something."

"Coffee is there," she nodded to the pot on the stove.

Perfect.

Henry detoured to the washroom-slash-utility room off the back of the kitchen to wash his own hands before he returned to the kitchen. He poured two mugs, leaving plenty of coffee for his brothers and their wives.

When he brought hers, Clara was wiping her hands on her apron, the cookies all lined up neatly on their pan.

Her eyes lit up with surprise as Henry held out the coffee to her. "Thank you," she murmured.

He pressed the coffee mug into her hand and then noticed the dusting of flour on the bridge of her nose.

"What?" she demanded.

He hadn't even realized he was smiling. The muscles in his cheek almost felt stiff from disuse.

"I think you were a casualty of the girls' wild baking..." His voice trailed off as he reached up to brush the white dust from her nose. He only touched her with one side of his thumb, only for a second, but Clara froze, wide-eyed. Was she even breathing?

The moment became charged as Henry realized how close they were standing, close enough that he could see the golden flecks in her hazel eyes, the spray of freckles he'd uncovered beneath that flour on her nose.

He could lean forward and kiss her. Especially if she kept looking at him like that—

A happy shriek from Maggie in the next room startled them both and the moment was broken.

Clara seemed to finally breathe again as she quickly turned away. Quick enough that coffee sloshed over the rim of her cup and dotted the floor.

He felt as if he couldn't breathe at all as she moved to open the oven door and place the two cookie sheets inside.

She wouldn't quite look at him as she began cleaning up.

Henry moved to help her, getting a wet rag to try to mop up the mess on the floor.

What was that?

He'd started this whole thing to get Mom off his back and to help out Clara, who he knew needed a friend.

But that bolt of attraction that had just passed between them had been the furthest thing from friendship.

Chapter Nine

A few days later, Henry was laying tile in the rental house bathroom. He'd done the worst of it, cutting and placing the tile pieces that went in the corners and along one side of the wall.

It was dusty, dirty work. His back and knees ached.

Henry took off the mask protecting his mouth and nose from dust when he went outside to tote in a heavy box of full-size square tiles. Stretching his back, he let the mask hang from his neck and stood next to the bed of his truck for a moment. He grabbed a water jug from the front seat of his truck and quenched his thirst.

The sun was about to set. Everything had that late afternoon golden hue to it. Like the other day, when he'd driven Clara home from David's house.

Movement from the crawl space caught his eye and he found his feet carrying him in that direction, a little grateful for the interruption to his thoughts. He was thinking about Clara far too much for the past few days.

Henry could hear a couple soft mewls and then silence as he approached. He stopped a few feet away, figuring it was better not to scare the mama or her babies.

Surely they were getting big enough now that he could call animal control.

Clara would hate that.

When Henry had stood there for a minute or so, the mama cat sauntered out of her crawl space and right up to his foot to sniff his work boot.

The cat looked exponentially better than when he'd first seen her. She'd gained a few ounces. Her hair was smooth and shiny—though she obviously still needed a bath.

Clara had done more than just kept her alive. She was on the cusp of thriving.

And there was Clara in his thoughts again.

The cat didn't twine through his legs, like he might've expected. She sat about a foot away from him and started cleaning a front paw.

"You need to find a home."

She ignored him in favor of swiping at her cheek with her now clean paw.

Henry sighed. The sound startled the cat into momentary stillness. Then she looked straight at him and then the house.

"This is not your home," he said.

What had he become, arguing with a cat?

But he let himself look at the peaceful surroundings. The farm across the road had been harvested last week. There was a beauty in the land that had grown crops, given a bounty this year. The farm Clara's great-aunt lived on was nearby, out of sight behind the house. It was smaller, but still had a lovely, peaceful feel to it.

He could picture Clara there, standing on the front porch of the house where he'd picked her up, surrounded on all sides by little kids. Girls and boys. He'd thought the other night how good she was with kids.

The guys in Hickory Harbor couldn't be that obtuse. Some Amish guy was bound to notice her, decide to court her, marry her.

That was her whole mission.

But ever since the other night, the thought of Clara marrying some Amish guy twisted him up inside. Henry wanted to date her. For real, not pretend.

It wasn't fair, because it wasn't like he was going to throw his hat in the ring. His engagement had become a disaster. Nell had broken his heart. His life had fallen apart. He never wanted to experience that type of loss again. He wasn't the guy for Clara and they both knew it.

But he hadn't figured on this whole fake dating thing getting complicated.

A vehicle was coming up the road and he was grateful for the distraction, until he realized it was his father's truck and Dad was slowing to turn into the driveway.

Henry glanced down to see the mama cat disappearing into her hidey-hole.

"Smart girl," he muttered.

He went to meet his dad, finding a smile from somewhere deep inside. "Hey."

Dad got out of the truck. "Henry. You look tired."

Henry brushed a hand through his hair. "Probably just tile dust." But that didn't stop him from standing up a little straighter. "You want to see inside?"

"Sure."

Henry felt like he was fifteen all over again, bringing home a wooden birdhouse from shop class for Dad's inspection. It had been his first solo project and he'd been nervous what Dad would say...

Right now Dad wasn't saying anything. He moved slowly through the open-concept living room to where Henry had demoed the upper half of the wall into the kitchen. Henry planned for a bigger countertop that would extend seating into the living room and make for a better entertaining space. But right now the cabinets were open on top, waiting for the slab of marble that wouldn't arrive for several weeks.

Henry liked how the room looked. It was way more open, and light from the big window above the kitchen sink illuminated all the way into the living room.

But Dad only glanced around and then moved past the kitchen and into the hall.

"You mom wants to know if you'll meet us for dinner one evening next week."

"Sure," Henry replied easily before Dad could say more. Specifically about whether Nell had contacted Mom again. Why wasn't Dad commenting on the work he'd done?

Dad glanced into the bedroom where Henry had had to put up new Sheetrock where the water damage had been uncovered. He still needed to texture and paint.

And then Dad stopped in the bathroom doorway where Henry had all his tools and a bucket of grout still lying out. "That the tile you chose?"

"Yep." Maybe his voice sounded a little tight but he couldn't seem to help it. The tile was a neutral gray that they'd used in several projects over the past year. Henry knew what paint colors would look best with it.

And finally Dad turned to look at Henry again, where he stood at the mouth of the hallway. "Looks like you're still a couple of days behind schedule."

Henry worked at keeping his expression neutral. "We both know that delays are part of the process, sometimes. The vandalism cost me a day's work to clean up and the water damage another. Don't worry. I plan to work a couple hours most evenings and I should be able to catch up."

Dad frowned, rather than look happy that Henry had everything in hand.

"I thought I heard you'd signed up for some volleyball team. Won't that eat into your work time?"

Dad must've talked to Todd already.

"I'll work things out. I promise." He still felt the weight of the mistakes he'd made eighteen months ago. He could understand why Dad might worry.

He wasn't going to go there.

Dad was already distracted, touching the doorjamb. "I'm considering retiring. I've got an offer. A decent one. Your mom thinks it's time."

Henry felt like he'd been hit by a car. For a fractured moment he couldn't find breath or words.

"I always thought I would take over the business," Henry said carefully at last, and continued, "I want to. I could go to the bank to see about a loan—"

Dad shook his head. "You'd be a good partner, not an owner. You're not ready."

Henry grew nauseated. This *was* about his past mistakes.

"I wish I had twenty more years to work with you. Mentor you. But your mom is right. It's time for me to slow down."

What was there to say to that?

Henry moved out of the way when Dad walked down the hallway and back to the front door.

"We can talk more at dinner." Henry didn't lift his head to acknowledge. "Your mom wants you to bring your Amish friend."

He left without waiting for Henry's answer. Which was good. All Henry could think about were his father's words. *You're not ready.*

His past failures would haunt him forever.

"Relax."

Clara was trying.

But Henry's kind demand did the opposite of what he asked.

Clara couldn't force herself to relax. Not when she was so out of her element.

The two of them arrived at the grassy field outside the community school for the first volleyball practice.

Why had she agreed to do this?

Henry parked his truck. At the same time, several Amish buggies pulled up. Two more players had ridden up on bicycles and then another buggy pulled up.

By the time Henry and Clara had gotten out of the truck and walked across the grassy field, she counted eight people. Two young men worked on setting up two separate volleyball nets right there on the grass.

"Come on," Henry murmured.

Unlike the other day when he'd taken her bike riding, tonight Henry didn't seem to register her nerves. He'd been distracted on the drive over, had barely said ten words.

Several young folks glanced curiously in Henry and Clara's direction as they approached the group. Henry seemed to take it in stride, nodding and even once calling out a hello.

When they stopped walking, Clara turned to face him. He had a volleyball between his hands and now tossed it into the air gently for her to bump back to him. Several other players were doing the same.

It was the presence of so many unfamiliar faces that made it difficult for Clara to concentrate.

It got worse when Abe and his brother joined the growing group. Lena had told Henry and Clara that there were at least two teams practicing together on Tuesday and Thursday evenings. She hadn't known Abe would be here.

A rogue ball flew through the air and whacked Henry on the back of one shoulder. He'd been right in the middle of a toss to Clara and she caught the ball instead of hitting it back to him.

He scooped up the bonus ball and tossed it to a young man in Amish garb who stood nearby with arms outstretched.

"I'm Henry Barrett," he introduced himself.

The young man gave his name—Aaron Beacon—and a handshake before trotting back to the young woman he'd been warming up with.

Introductions seemed to come easy to Henry, who faced her again and motioned that he was ready for the ball.

Meanwhile, Clara's heart was pounding in her ears. She felt shaky and a little sick to her stomach. What was she even doing here? Making a fool out of herself?

How was being terrible at volleyball supposed to win her a husband?

"Bump it like we practiced at the house," Henry suggested kindly.

But when he tossed the ball to her again, she hit it far too hard and it sailed over his head. Was it…? It rolled toward Abe and his warm-up partner.

She couldn't watch.

She put her face in her hands as a blush flamed in her cheeks.

"Hi, Clara." Lena's chipper greeting had her pulling her hands down from her face.

Todd was right behind his wife, answering a greeting that someone had called out to him. It seemed everyone knew the town doctor. Lena, too.

And then Lena gave Clara a brief hug. It was so unexpected that she forgot for a moment that everyone was probably staring at them—at her. Wondering who she was and why Lena was hugging her.

Clara let it all go for a moment and enjoyed the surprising affection.

"Hey, Lena!" Two young women waved and approached as Henry and Todd exchanged words. Henry had the ball tucked beneath his arm and looked like he was fuming. What was going on?

When Henry had helped her out of the truck minutes ago, she'd tried not to notice how his blue T-shirt seemed to hug the muscles in his shoulders and arms.

She'd noticed.

"This is my friend Clara."

She blinked out of her thoughts, warmth buzzing beneath her skin, and realized Lena was introducing her. She met Laurie and Cynthia Anders, who welcomed her warmly.

When Laura leaned in to ask Lena something, Cynthia turned to Clara.

"I'm nervous," Cynthia confessed. "I've never played volleyball before."

"Me, too!" Clara stumbled over her agreement. "I mean, I'm nervous, too. I've never played any sport."

Cynthia didn't seem to mind that Clara's nerves had turned her into a babbling brook.

And then someone gave a loud whistle and individual conversations died down as everyone grouped up around a tall guy Clara recognized from house church. She couldn't recall his name.

And then Henry was there, joining the group just behind her. When Clara turned to check he was there, he gently nudged her elbow with his. He had the ball between his hands.

The young man in charge started explaining how the practice would work.

Henry leaned in to whisper in her ear, "You're being too

hard on yourself. Expecting too much. Think back to the very first time you made cookies."

She wanted to tell him to shush. Surely his whispering was disrupting the players nearby. But it was Lena who was watching, with a tiny knowing smile.

Clara dropped her eyes.

Henry wasn't finished. "You probably read and reread the recipe five or six times while you made your first batch of cookies."

He was right.

Clara must've been eight or nine, and though they rarely had sweets, she'd begged Grandma to let her bake cookies.

The cookies hadn't even tasted good. But Clara had tried again, this time following the recipe to the letter. That one success had given her confidence—in her baking, at least.

"Just follow the instructions," Henry said, with a nod to the guy who'd finished telling them about the upcoming tournament and was now explaining how each week's practices would work.

It couldn't be that easy.

But when Clara and Henry's team was divided into its own group, and Abe was across the field, on the other team, she felt a beat of relief. At least if she made a fool of herself, he'd be farther away. Maybe he wouldn't even see.

Their practice was led by a teammate who'd played before, and was a good teacher. Soon enough, Clara's muscles had become warm and loose and she was making the ball go where it was supposed to. Mostly.

It was hard to be self-conscious when Henry whispered, "Nice hit!" as they passed each other, moving through a rotation on their grassy court.

And when she managed to get a serve over the net, Henry smiled at her with such warmth in his expression that her stomach flipped over. Whatever his distraction had been earlier, talking with Todd seemed to have solved it.

Henry was moved to the opposite side of the net as practice continued, and she found herself in position with Lena at one side.

"Henry can't keep his eyes off you," Lena whispered. "It's cute."

Clara missed the next ball, an easy one that was in her quadrant of the court. Her team called out encouragement as she moved back into a ready position.

But she couldn't stop thinking about Lena's whisper.

Lena had been genuinely kind to her. She'd introduced Clara to her real friends and now... Clara and Henry were deceiving her. And Todd.

Clara had shoved away her misgivings in the beginning, believing that the ends would justify the means. She wanted a family. Wanted a husband to cherish her.

But now Clara couldn't help but wonder what it was going to cost. She didn't like the guilt twisting her insides at the thought of deceiving Lena. She was the first real friend Clara had made since she'd come to live in Hickory Harbor. Other than Henry, and he didn't count.

After practice had concluded and they'd said their goodbyes, Henry drove her home.

He was quiet again, like he'd been on the drive to practice.

She considered bringing up their deception but hadn't gotten the first words past her lips when he pulled up in the drive.

"Thanks for taking me." Clara took the coward's way out and jumped from the truck before he could say anything.

She darted up the steps and into Dorcas's house, leaning against the door once she'd closed it.

Loneliness wrapped around her like a shawl. There was no light left on. There was little chance Dorcas had left her a plate from dinner.

It couldn't be wrong to desire someone to care about her. To look forward to her being home. To care that she had enough to eat, to tell about her day.

Henry's plan could work.

But would her deception cost her the new friendship she was forging with Lena?

Chapter Ten

Practice rolled around again two days later. This time, Henry had asked if he and Clara could pick up Todd and Lena along the way, which meant more company in the truck.

The practice went better than he expected. Clara had found a tiny spark of confidence. She greeted several players on their team and everyone had been friendly and kind.

He hadn't missed the way two of the men had looked at Clara. Their gazes had held clear interest. That was good for her plan, right? But for some reason, it made his chest tight.

After practice was over, all four of them piled in his truck again. Henry was smiling as he listened to Lena and Clara chatting from the back seat. He caught a glance from Todd, a knowing rise of his eyebrows.

They hadn't gone far down the road when Henry's cell phone rang from the console.

It was an unknown number and he silenced the call.

But when the phone rang a second time, Henry frowned and picked it up, keeping one eye on the empty two-lane road.

"Here," Todd said. "I got you."

He handed the phone to his brother without looking. Trusting Todd was something he would've done as a teenager, when Todd was in college, back when they'd been close.

It wasn't until Todd had tapped the button to answer the phone that Henry had second thoughts.

What if it was Nell on the line, calling from a different phone?

"Hello?" It was only a moment before Todd glanced over. "It's David."

The women went silent in the back seat.

He wasn't aware that David even had his phone number. Ruby's due date was close. Was it the baby?

"Yes," Todd said into the phone. "Keep her lying down."

Henry caught Todd's worried glance but he was already activating the blinker, checking traffic—there was none—and slowing to make a U-turn right in the road. David and Ruby's house was two miles in the other direction.

Todd made a hand motion that Henry interpreted as *hurry.*

Lena sat forward in her seat and rested her hand on Todd's shoulder. Henry felt a prick of some emotion—envy?—at watching the intimate moment of comfort.

He glanced in the rearview mirror. The road behind him was still empty, but he caught Clara's concerned gaze before he returned his eyes to the road.

"We've got Henry and Clara with us. We'll figure something out. We're three minutes away. All right."

It was awful, only hearing one side of the conversation and feeling this uncertainty. What was going on?

Todd spoke in quick sentences as he dug beneath the seat for the black doctor's bag he stashed there when Henry and Clara had picked up the other couple.

"Ruby's gone into labor. There might be complications. He was too worried to give me specifics. I'll need to check her out first thing."

Todd glanced at Henry. "I'm glad you were driving. It would've taken much longer to get over here in a buggy."

Henry didn't have a chance to ask how David had gotten his cell phone number before they pulled into the drive.

He was still shutting off the truck when Todd jumped out.

"Go." Lena shooed him from the back seat. She struggled with the handle to slide the seat forward and Henry jogged around the front of the truck to help her out as Todd ran up the porch steps.

"Thanks," Lena said as Henry handed her out.

He stood there, staring at Clara, who looked wide-eyed and a little nervous.

"Should we go in?" she asked hesitantly.

Henry didn't know. He didn't want to be in the way.

But Lena had barely made the door when she leaned back out and waved at them.

"Guess that's our answer."

He helped Clara out of the truck, giving his best attempt at ignoring the spike of warmth when his hand clasped hers briefly.

Lena met them at the door. "Can you distract the girls?"

The girls? It was a moment before he realized Mindy and Maggie were in the living room. It had to be past Maggie's bedtime but both girls had tears on their cheeks and were standing in the middle of the room.

"Of course," Clara said. She brushed past him and moved to crouch in front of the girls. "Do you remember me? My name is Clara."

Mindy nodded while Maggie only sniffled.

"*Mamm*'s havin' the baby and she's hurt," Mindy said.

Henry glanced where Lena had been moments ago but she had already gone up the stairs to the second floor. What were they supposed to say to that?

He moved to stand behind the couch, awkward and unsure.

"It's a very good thing your *onkle* Todd is a doctor. He's here to help your *mamm*." Clara pointed to several children's books laid out on the coffee table. "Were you reading books before bed? Do you want to read with me?"

Maggie nodded, easily moving toward Clara with her arms raised, asking to be lifted onto the couch. Clara sat down beside her, but when she reached out a hand for Mindy, the older girl shook her head and rounded the arm of the couch.

Clara smiled. "That's okay." She picked up one of the books and showed the cover to Maggie, who nodded.

Mindy stayed where she was, near the arm of the couch, and Henry stayed where he was, watching from behind. Clara's sweet, soothing voice read the words on the pages.

And then there were voices and then movement from the upstairs hallway and Todd came down the stairs first.

He approached Henry and spoke in a low voice, eyes flicking to the little girls. "Ruby needs to go to the hospital. Her blood pressure is high and she'll get the best care there. Better than what Lena and I can provide at the birthing center."

"What do you need from me?"

Todd gave a tired, chagrined smile. "It'll take longer for an ambulance to arrive…"

"Take my truck," Henry said when he realized what his brother was hinting at. "You remember how to drive…?" He pressed the keys into Todd's hand.

Todd rolled his eyes and nudged his brother. "Thank you."

A few minutes later, Ruby walked down the stairs, assisted by David on one side and Lena on the other.

"What about the girls?" Ruby asked David. "Your *mamm* and *daed* aren't home—"

"Your family will come," David said gently.

"And we'll stay until she does," Clara added from her place on the couch.

Ruby looked relieved. She must love the girls very much if she was worried about them at this moment, when she was in obvious distress. She didn't protest again as she was led out the front door.

David hesitated at the threshold, then came back to press a kiss on both girl's heads. "We will be back soon, with a little *boppli* brother or sister."

Maggie was already leaning over the page with Clara, but Mindy watched him go with a trembling lip. Henry didn't know what to do.

David left, closing the door behind him.

Clara just kept reading. That first book, then a second one that had Maggie clapping and giggling.

By the third book, he wondered whether he should get Clara a glass of water. Surely her throat had to be drying up after all that.

But then he noticed that Mindy shifted slightly closer, coming behind the corner of the couch.

Clara seemed to notice, too, as she tilted the book slightly so that it would be easier for Mindy to see.

At the next book change, Mindy scooted more toward Henry.

In the middle of the book, her little hand slipped into his.

He must've made some noise, because Clara glanced up for a moment where their eyes met and held. Warmth spread through him.

Henry barely knew his nieces. But in this moment, that didn't matter. They were family.

That small shift made for a change in the whole evening. Mindy and Maggie had a cup of warm milky tea with

Clara, and then all four trooped upstairs and he and Clara tucked the girls in.

The two tots must've been tired from the excitement and nerves, because it wasn't long before they nodded off.

Back in the kitchen, Clara started cleaning up. Henry moved to the living room to pick up all the books they'd scattered.

A tone from his phone alerted him and he thought maybe it was Todd. It was a voice mail from a blocked number. It had to be Nell.

He stuffed his phone in his pocket, glancing into the kitchen where Clara was humming softly to herself while she scrubbed dishes in the sink.

She was nothing like Nell. Nell would've agreed to watch the girls, but she would've sent him resentful looks all night because their plans had been interrupted.

Why had Henry ignored Nell's self-centered nature for so long?

Clara hadn't hesitated, jumping in when she was needed.

She glanced over her shoulder and caught him watching. Henry moved into the kitchen and found a towel to dry with.

"How did you know that reading would calm them down?" he asked.

"I didn't." She didn't look at him as she scrubbed the mug Mindy had used for her apple juice. "I haven't been around kids much. I was making it up as I went along. I've always loved stories and I thought they might, too."

Henry huffed a laugh, and when she smiled up at him, he was hit with a punch of affection.

He liked her.

The moment passed and Clara handed him the mug, leaving him to stew in his thoughts.

He'd told her—told himself—he wasn't interested in dating again after Nell.

But if he was interested, Clara would definitely be someone that attracted him.

But she had a specific kind of husband in mind. An Amish one.

And Henry was only in Hickory Harbor a few more weeks, until he finished the house project.

Nothing could come of this.

It was mighty inconvenient for him to realize she might be a perfect match for him.

Clara walked home next to Henry well after nightfall.

Ruby's brother Evan and sister-in-law Beth had arrived soon after they'd cleaned up the kitchen.

After dropping off Beth, Evan had driven both of them to Clara's home in his buggy. She'd asked to be dropped off at the drive, just in case the noise of the horses and carriage woke up Dorcas.

Henry had insisted on walking her to the door.

There was a part of Clara that wished it had taken longer for Evan and Beth to arrive. She and Henry had spent time after they'd tucked in the girls tidying up and talking.

Henry was easy to talk to.

Except he was quiet now. She knew he had worked all morning, then gone to volleyball practice and then helped out at David and Ruby's. He had to be exhausted from a long day.

It was she who felt jittery and energized from being with him. She couldn't help notice an awareness of him walking beside her with his confident stride.

As they approached Dorcas's house, she saw there were lamps lit in the living room window. That was different. Was her great-aunt waiting up? Why?

The thought twisted her stomach. She wasn't hiding her friendship with Henry, wasn't purposely sneaking around. But her great-aunt had strong views about *Englishers* and Clara wanted this friendship with Henry.

Her worries flew out of her mind when Henry's stride stuttered.

He took something from his pocket, and she saw the light from his cell phone illuminate his face briefly before he answered the phone with a low, gruff, "Hello?"

He touched Clara's wrist, the simple brush of his fingers enough to stop her forward movement.

Henry moved the phone away from his mouth momentarily to whisper, "It's Todd."

She felt the tension in him as they stood in darkness beneath the starry sky.

She'd seen his tension earlier, too, as Ruby had come down the stairs, white-faced and clearly in pain.

Henry had been worried about his sister-in-law.

Now he listened for a few moments, standing close as if he didn't realize he had leaned into Clara's personal space.

Clara strained her ears, but couldn't make out individual words coming from Henry's phone. She wanted to know if Ruby and the baby were okay.

"Thanks for letting me know." His voice was rough with emotion. He took the phone from his ear, tapped the screen a couple of times and then it went dark, too. He dropped his hand.

"Ruby had the baby. A little boy. Timothy James. They're both doing fine."

He was so near that Clara felt the tension rush out of him, even as the emotion in his words registered.

She didn't know who reached for who, but it was the

most natural thing in the world to slip her arms around his waist as he pulled her into a hug.

Henry was a good hugger. She felt safe in the circle of his arms. Wanted.

Was this true friendship?

And then he edged back slightly, enough that she could look up in the faint starlight and see his face.

He was so close.

For a breathless moment, she thought he meant to kiss her.

But somewhere in one of the rooms on Dorcas's second floor, a light went on. The small amount of extra illumination, echoed outside, was enough interference for the moment to be broken. Henry stepped back, his arms falling away from her.

"Thank you for everything tonight. Helping with the girls, and…everything."

She'd never heard him so discombobulated. He must be relieved for David, about Ruby.

"I'm glad I was there," she said.

He seemed to hesitate and she was breathless with wondering if he would say more. But he backed away.

As Henry trudged up the driveway the direction he'd come, Clara's heart panged to see him go.

"I'll see you on Sunday?" she called.

"Yeah. G'night."

"Goodbye."

She slipped inside and stood next to the door as she imagined him walking away, getting in Evan's buggy. Going home.

Her heart was still flying from that moment of closeness. What did it mean?

She startled when she turned away from the door and

came face-to-face with Dorcas. Clara pressed her hand to her racing heart. "You gave me a fright."

"You're late. Who was that?" Dorcas demanded. Her voice was shaky. "Who dropped you off?"

Clara turned her head toward the door, though it was silly as she couldn't see Henry anymore. "A friend."

Was Henry only a friend? That moment they'd shared outside—that had meant something. Hadn't it?

"An *Englisher* friend?" Her great-aunt said the words with more coldness in her voice than Clara had ever heard from her. "Martha told me she'd seen you talking to an *Englisher* after house church."

"Henry Barrett is the doctor's brother. David Weiss, too." Everyone in town knew the connection.

Dorcas coughed, the sound harsh and cutting. "He's an *Englisher*."

So he was.

Todd had joined the Amish church.

But earlier tonight, Henry had offhandedly mentioned that he didn't think he could ever give up his truck, or his phone, to live a simple Amish life.

"Your mother was foolish enough to fall for an *Englisher*. She was shunned for it."

Clara felt the warning words like a slap. It was her father that Dorcas was talking about. Her memories of her parents were so distant…but she remembered the love they shared. The laughter.

Her father had been a good man, even if he hadn't been a part of the Amish church or belonged to this community.

"Henry and I are just friends," she repeated.

"Then why sneak around?" Dorcas demanded. "Your cousin was over for supper tonight and she said you'd been seeing him for weeks."

This very moment was why Clara had wildly hoped that Dorcas never found out.

Clara was shaking with nerves at the confrontation. She fisted her hands in her skirt.

"I told you about joining the volleyball team," she said. Her emotions felt ragged. Her great-aunt must care about her. That had to be where this concern stemmed from. But every word from Dorcas felt like an attack. "Henry has been giving me rides, since I can't drive a buggy." *It was your idea for me to make friends.* She only shouted the words inside her own head.

Clara's trembling grew until her whole body was shaking, and to her horror, she felt a tear slip down one cheek.

"You don't understand how difficult it's been for me to fit in, to make friends."

Dorcas scowled. "How is an *Englisher* going to help you make friends? Except with his own kind?"

Dorcas didn't understand. And she didn't seem to want to.

"I'm tired," Clara said. "I'm going to bed." She passed her great-aunt on trembling legs.

Dorcas called up the stairs after her. "You shouldn't see him again."

"He's my ride," Clara said. She hurried up the stairs, afraid to look back and see her great-aunt's reaction to her words. Her heart pounded wildly, drumming in her ears.

Had she ever stood up to the woman before?

Your mother was shunned.

Had Dorcas been trying to warn her? Would she really turn Clara out for being friends with Henry?

Henry had been the only one on her side. He'd encouraged the volleyball idea. Had helped her gain more confidence.

He'd drawn her out of the terrible, lonely place she'd been in when they'd met.

In the darkness of her room, Clara shut the door and leaned on it.

Dorcas was only worried that Clara was going to fall in love with Henry and leave. She was a crotchety, lonely old woman.

But Clara's thoughts strayed to those breathless moments standing outside beside Henry.

Would he have kissed Clara if Dorcas hadn't turned on the light?

Did she want his kiss?

Was her great-aunt right after all? Maybe Clara was like her mother.

Chapter Eleven

Clara watched the scenery go by as Henry drove her home from practice a week later.

Compared to the week before, she felt as if she'd barely seen Henry. Dorcas had claimed to be sick on Sunday morning and asked Clara to stay home with her. For over an hour, the older woman had sat knitting on the couch while Clara read aloud from the Bible.

There'd been practice on Tuesday evening, but Henry had come straight from work and seemed distracted the entire time.

Tonight, Henry had received a phone call as he parked the truck. He'd motioned her to go on to practice while he'd taken the call.

He was quiet again, and Clara stole glances at him as he drove. She didn't know what to do with the invisible strands of tension that crisscrossed the air between them.

He spoke at last. "You played well tonight."

Clara pulled a face and he chuckled. "You did. I wish you could see the improvement in yourself since that first night."

She still felt awkward and slow, but she had hit several balls over the net when they'd flown in her direction. She was beginning to get the rhythm of the game.

"Did you have fun?" Henry asked.

She considered for a moment. "Yes." It was true. When had she stopped worrying so much about what everyone thought and making a fool of herself? Without that weight pressing down on her constantly, Clara made less missteps, smiled more.

Volleyball practice was fun.

Clara wouldn't confess that she'd attempted to ride the bike again, this time in Dorcas's backyard. It had not gone any better than the first time. She felt as if she didn't have enough limbs or maybe not enough focus to make everything move at the same time. Pedals, steer, balance. She'd scraped her elbow, but the wound didn't show beneath the sleeve of her dress.

"What about you? Did you have fun?" she asked him.

They'd spent nearly a month with Henry pretending to be romantically interested in her. She'd begun to wonder when he would tire of the whole thing.

"I always have fun when I'm with you."

Clara wanted to believe his easy words, and she didn't want to examine too deeply why that was.

She liked Henry.

"I saw you and Abe talking, during the warm-ups."

He'd still been standing beside his truck, talking on the phone, while she exchanged hellos with some of the young women from the team. She'd slowly begun to feel as if she was making acquaintances that had the potential to become friends.

Still, she'd been surprised when Abe had been the one to approach her and ask to bump the ball around before practice officially started.

"What did the two of you talk about?" Henry's question seemed innocent enough. He was relaxed in his seat, hands clasped loosely on the wheel. He seemed genuinely curious, though there was a tension she couldn't understand buzzing beneath the surface.

"I don't know." Clara's mind felt fuzzy trying to recall those flustered moments when she'd been trying not to trip over her own feet and gently bump the ball while making conversation. "How nice the weather has been. Whether we're looking forward to the tournament." The tournament was in a little over a week. Abe was excited about it, but Clara was nervous that she'd mess up during a real game and lose points for her team.

Quiet descended in the cab between them; it felt somehow thicker this time.

When Henry spoke again, his voice was subdued somehow. "Did you ask him whether he was going to the upcoming singing?"

She shook her head. "I didn't think of it. Everything happened so quickly and I was—" *Flustered.* She didn't say it, but Henry nodded as if he'd heard her anyway.

If Clara had thought of it, she didn't know that she would've had the courage to say anything.

"You don't have anything to worry about, you know." Henry said the words in a matter-of-fact way. "He wouldn't have come over to talk to you if he wasn't interested."

She wasn't sure about that. Why would Abe—or anyone else—be interested in her?

"Just be yourself. You're special, Clara."

His words made warmth bloom in her sternum and flow up into her face.

Henry believed in her. Believed that Abe would be interested in her. She wanted—

"Maybe next time, you should bring a plate of your cookies. They'll for sure win the heart of any guy around."

She laughed, as he'd meant her to, though she was shaking her head.

"I'm not kidding."

Clara's cookies may have been great, but he was teasing her, and they both knew it.

Being with Henry was effortless. That was the thought that had been spinning in her head once practice had begun and her few moments with Abe were over. Lena and Todd and the rest of her team had formed a small huddle, and Henry had joined just as their team leader and unofficial coach had begun to speak.

When Clara would've stood awkwardly at the edge of the huddle, Henry had come beside her and nudged her forward with a gentle hand to her lower back. Anna, one of the other girls, had shuffled to the side so Clara could be a part of the group.

Because of Henry. He had to have known she wouldn't have stepped forward on her own.

Other than the bike incident, they worked together seamlessly.

"Are we going to stop and check on your mama kitty?" The words had a breathless quality when Clara asked them. She didn't want her time with Henry to be over. Not yet.

He hesitated slightly. "Sure. And she's not my cat. Couple more weeks and the kittens will be big enough to move. We'll find them a good home."

He slowed the truck and turned into the driveway, but stopped abruptly before they'd gotten close to the house.

"What's wrong?" She loosened the seat belt from where it'd locked at his sudden stop.

"I don't know—I think the front door is open."

His headlights cut through the near darkness, and sure

enough, the shadows thrown made it look like the front door was ajar. She squinted. Was it…?

Before Henry could get out of the still-running truck, she grabbed his shirtsleeve. "The doorjamb is busted. Don't."

Don't what? Go inside? Put himself in danger? Clara didn't know what she meant to say, only that a strong urgency for him to stay right where he was gripped her.

The doorjamb was broken, a long strip hanging loose, just above the lock. As if someone had taken a pry bar to it.

A muscle jumped in Henry's cheek. "I'll call the police and then take you home."

It didn't take long for him to make the phone call. She wanted to check on the mama and kittens but knew better than to approach the house right now. What if someone dangerous was still inside?

Henry was silent as he backed out of the driveway and took the turn to take her home. He was upset. And he had a right to be. Who would break in? She didn't know what they'd done inside, whether they'd stolen anything.

But whatever it was, it couldn't be good.

There were no lights on at Dorcas's house and Clara's heart sank. She didn't want a confrontation, but she also didn't want to walk inside to darkness.

She got out of the truck, anyway, as Henry rounded the front of the vehicle.

"Thank you for driving me." She almost winced at the inane words. She could see his thoughts were back at the house. His jaw was set and his eyes were dark.

She wanted to reach out and hug him.

But she didn't.

She just awkwardly waved and went inside the house.

Alone.

* * *

Henry watched Clara go inside, feeling a strange detachment as he did.

It was a stark contrast to the jealousy that had streaked through his belly earlier. First, when Abe had spent several minutes giving her obviously easy tosses and smiling at her as they'd chatted. And again when Henry had brought up the interaction in the truck.

Henry could see what Clara couldn't. Abe would be stupid not to see how kind and warmhearted she was. And beautiful.

Henry drove off from her house trying to shake free of thoughts that weren't going to help him right now.

He'd only been parked in the driveway for a minute or so when a police cruiser turned in behind him, lights off.

He didn't want to go inside.

But this was his project, and he had to.

The policeman asked for a moment to make sure the house was empty, and Henry was left staring at the outside of the structure in the dark.

Two break-ins couldn't be random, could they? It had to be the same person. Or people.

Why were the vandals targeting Henry? Was it simply because no one lived in the house yet? Because it was clearly empty when Henry wasn't working on it?

Or was it something more sinister?

The officer came outside and motioned for Henry to follow him inside.

"There's some damage that I'll make a note of. You want to look around and tell me if anything's missing? Tools, maybe?"

Henry's temper flared when he crossed to the unfinished kitchen, where he'd left a compressor and nail gun and a toolbox with his expensive battery-powered drill and tools he'd carried for years. He'd thought they were safe because the house was locked and secure.

He told the officer, who noted it in a notebook.

"I'm gonna take a look around outside," the officer said.

And Henry was left to walk through the interior. Someone had kicked in the Sheetrock in several places in the hallway and one bedroom. They'd broken the mirror he'd hung in the almost-finished bathroom.

Why would anyone cause unnecessary damage like this on purpose?

Henry's stomach twisted when he entered the master bedroom and saw that whoever had done this had opened one of his paint cans and kicked it over, and drying paint now covered almost ten square feet of the wood floor he'd painstakingly laid.

He ran to the kitchen and found some builders rags and a plastic trash bag. He was down on his knees mopping up what he could when the policeman returned.

"You make anybody mad lately?"

Henry scowled at the floor. "I've been working and minding my own business. I barely know anyone in town."

"Quite a mess."

Henry had managed to wipe up some of the liquid to keep it from spreading, but there was a huge stain on the floor of paint that had already seeped into the wood and stained.

"Any ideas who might've done this?" Henry asked, trying to keep his voice tight and not lose control. Anger made his hands shake and it wasn't the officer's fault. "Some troublemaking teens maybe?"

"Whoever it was didn't leave muddy footprints leading to their hideout." Was that sarcasm?

Henry pinched his lips together.

"I don't suppose you've got a security camera or one of those doorbells?" the officer asked.

Henry shook his head. He hadn't thought he'd needed one. Hickory Harbor was supposed to be safe.

"I'll do some digging, give you a call when I've made some progress."

But Henry wasn't holding his breath. No one had called him about the earlier break-in and vandalism. When Henry had phoned the police station for an update a week ago, there'd been no progress on the case.

The officer left and Henry finished what he could do with the paint.

He took the soiled rags and plastic out to the trash and stood in the dark, hands hanging at his sides.

In the past, he would've called his dad. Dad would've known what to do.

But Dad wanted to sell the business. Henry wanted to show him that he could handle things.

He just didn't know how to handle this.

He took his phone out of his pocket and dialed Todd's number at the birthing center, where his brother and Lena lived. There was a landline there.

"Hello?" Todd sounded professional and alert when he answered.

"Hey. It's me."

"Everything okay?"

Henry heard the murmur of Lena's voice in the background and Todd's returning words, "It's Henry."

He closed his eyes, pinching the bridge of his nose. "Yeah. Everything's okay." He couldn't tell Todd about the break-in. Todd had a busy, thriving medical practice and a new wife. He wasn't a builder.

"You wanna have lunch this week? If you can fit me in to your schedule?" Henry asked.

"We're doing lunch for David and Ruby and the kids on Wednesday. You said you'd come," Todd reminded him.

"Yeah, I'll be there." Henry had forgotten about the lunch. He'd meant to ask Clara to come with him, be a buffer. His mom kept asking about her.

"Are you sure you're okay? Something you need to talk about? Maybe Clara?"

"No. Clara's fine." She was off-limits. He couldn't tell his brother about his conflicting feelings because Todd didn't know.

"Something going on at the build?"

Henry swallowed his urge to tell Todd. "Nothing I can't handle."

The new damage and missing tools would be covered by Dad's builders' insurance policy, but he knew what dealing with insurance companies could be like. They'd delay and have adjusters out and ask questions and Henry would have to chase the money. Meanwhile the clock was ticking down for the house to be finished.

After everything, Henry had to prove himself to Dad if he wanted a chance at the business.

With the new damage to fix, he'd be working late into the night and every moment of the weekends. Did he even have time to compete in the volleyball tournament?

He'd promised Clara his help.

Henry didn't have answers. He rang off with Todd, promising to attend the lunch on Wednesday, and shoved his phone in his pocket, throat thick with despair.

He had no one to share this difficulty with.

A shadow moved at the end of the driveway, behind his

truck, and he whirled on his heel. Was that the vandal, back for more?

It was a young woman in a dress. One that he recognized as she entered the circle of light thrown by the overhead porch lamp.

Clara.

He strode to her, heart pounding. "What are you doing here? You walked all this way?"

Her chin jutted up in independence. "I wanted to check on you. And I'm used to walking."

"It's dangerous." He barely registered the concern in his voice, but felt it in every cell of his body.

"I wanted to make sure you were all right."

Her words registered and on top of the worry bubbling inside him, he did the only thing that seemed right. He crossed the last bit of space separating them and pulled her into his arms.

Clara wrapped her arms around his middle, easily sinking into his embrace.

Holding her felt right.

Henry breathed her in, a sweet smell of simple soap and something that must be Clara herself. She fit in his arms just right.

He wanted her closer.

When she tipped her head up, he found his right hand threading into her hair at the nape of her neck. He was probably dislodging the prayer *kapp* she always wore…

He dipped his head and—

Reality slammed into him.

He took one cleansing breath and a half step back, changing his hold so that their hands were clasped between them.

She looked up at him with luminous eyes.

One tug. That's all it would take and Clara would be back in his arms.

"I'm not sure this is a good idea. Kissing you," he added when a hint of confusion crossed her expressive face.

Her eyes widened slightly but she remained silent.

"Our arrangement was supposed to be—"

"What if we changed the arrangement?" she interrupted in a whisper.

How was he supposed to think straight in the face of her words, laced with hope and vulnerability?

He liked Clara. He wanted more.

But she trusted him, he reminded himself. She'd asked for his help. And kissing her would change everything.

"I think—" he hesitated but made himself finish the thought "—that changing our arrangement can't be something we decide in the heat of the moment. Can we…can we take some time? I want to make sure this is the right thing for both of us."

Clara's expression softened and he kicked himself for not just taking this chance.

But he couldn't hurt her. She meant too much.

Chapter Twelve

❧

"I'd like to recruit a nurse practitioner," Todd said.

Henry sipped from his coffee as Dad nodded along with his brother's statement.

The three of them sat on couches set up in a U-shape in the open sitting area in Lena's birthing center. The birthing center was a sprawling house that had been converted to something of a small-town hospital, though without most of the electronic gadgets one would find there. When a woman was having her baby, she could come here and have the baby and be cared for in those first critical days.

Today, Todd and Lena had set up a long folding table, covered with a pale blue cloth, in the waiting area. They lived in a bedroom off the back of the birthing center, so that Lena—and now Todd—could be ready to help a mother at any time, night or day.

The moment Henry and Clara had walked inside, Mindy and Maggie flocked to Clara. She'd laughed as they had pulled her by the hand to the kitchen. She'd been prepared for them, carrying a plain wicker basket in the crook of one arm.

Mom and Dad had picked up the girls earlier to give David and Ruby and the new baby some time alone, to rest for the day.

Mom and Lena moved back and forth between the

kitchen and sitting room, setting the table and carrying dishes.

Henry could hear the murmur of Mindy's voice and Clara's occasional response. Every once in a while, there was an urgent, happy statement from Maggie.

Henry tuned back in to the conversation Dad and Todd were having about the busy medical practice.

"...someone to handle the patient load if I get called away to assist Lena with a birth."

"You should see if your grandfather knows anyone looking to relocate," Mom said as she passed from the kitchen into the sitting room, carrying a basket of fluffy biscuits.

Henry's stomach gurgled when it registered the floury, yeasty scent.

Todd's gaze flicked to meet Henry's. A muscle jumped in his cheek like he was clamping down on his back teeth.

"Grandfather still needs time to come around," Dad said.

Mom glanced up and then back down at the table with a shake of her head.

"I'm sure I can find someone on my own," Todd muttered.

When Todd had made the decision to give up his job as an emergency room doctor to practice at the clinic in Hickory Harbor, Grandfather had disowned him. It didn't seem to bother Todd—usually.

But today, Todd seemed thoughtful and slightly hurt.

Lena moved behind her husband and touched his shoulder as she passed. Todd's gaze shifted to his wife and a hint of a smile appeared.

Henry hadn't understood at first, when Todd seemed to give up his entire life to move here and join the Amish church. But he was thriving in a more old-fashioned world, one without technology and with a strong community that rallied around his young family. And it couldn't be more obvious that he was deeply in love with Lena.

"We're thinking of building a house out behind the center," Todd said, distracted as he watched his wife move plates around at the table. "A little more room for the two of us, and our family when God decides to bless us with little ones. Don't get excited, Mom."

Mom laughed. "Don't get my hopes up. You know I'd love more grandchildren."

Todd turned his attention to Henry. "What would you think about staying and building our house after your current project wraps?"

Dad looked away, pretending to focus out the window into the front yard.

Henry set his coffee on a small end table nearby, pretending to focus on it while he felt the attention of the room shift to him.

"That'll depend on Dad. I might not have a job by then."

Todd's eyebrows crunched together, revealing his confusion.

Dad frowned. "Nobody said anything about you being out of a job." His voice was sharp.

"Michael," Mom said from the table.

"Dad's selling the business," Henry said to Todd.

His brother's eyes widened. "Since when?"

"It isn't a done deal," Dad said. "But your mother and I think it's time. The issues with my heart are resolved but I'd like more time to spend with my grandchildren."

He tipped his head and Henry noted the giggles from his nieces, in the kitchen with Clara.

"I thought Henry was going to take over when you retired." Todd's voice was laced with genuine curiosity.

Henry's breath froze in his lungs.

Dad tried to hem and haw, but when Todd stared expectantly, he finally said, "Henry doesn't need to be running a business."

The reminder that Henry had caused the loss with the Dudley project was like a slap. There was a sudden silence in the room, or maybe it was just Henry's ears that were ringing.

If he hadn't made such an incredible mistake, maybe the business could've been his.

His chest squeezed tight and he thought about walking out the front door, getting into his truck and just leaving.

He couldn't sit here—

At that moment, Mindy ran into the room. "Clara says we need you," she said breathlessly.

Mindy grabbed his hand and gave a tug, and through his numbness, Henry let her drag him toward the kitchen. He avoided his dad's and brother's eyes, heard the murmur of Mom's voice as he left the room.

He'd spent the first decade of his adult life pouring himself into Dad's business. Trying to prove that he was good enough.

But he hadn't been.

Henry's thoughts were still swirling as Mindy dragged him into the kitchen, until he caught sight of Clara.

Her apron was dotted with yellow batter and there was what looked like powdered sugar on her hands—and plenty on the countertop where Maggie stood on a chair, "helping."

Clara's eyes were dancing and none of his troubles disappeared, but he felt their hold on him slip.

"*Onkle* Henwy!" Maggie chirped.

Henry stepped into the sunlit room, letting go of Mindy to reach over and ruffle Maggie's hair.

"What are you doing in here, squirt? Other than making a mess?"

"Wemons!" Maggie crowed.

"We made lemon bars," Mindy said.

Clara swept some of the powdered sugar off the counter and into her hands, then moved toward the sink to deposit it there.

"We need you to taste test," Mindy said.

"Oh, yeah?" That didn't sound like they'd needed him, not really.

But Clara tossed over her shoulder, "It's a very important job."

"That so?"

She pointed to a tiny dessert plate out on the counter, where a yellow square dusted with powdered sugar waited for him.

"C'mon, *Onkle* Henry!" Mindy said.

"All right, all right." Dessert before lunch? Count him in.

Henry picked up the treat and took a bite, exaggerating every motion as the little girls' eyes were glued to him.

"Mmm," he hummed his approval long and loud.

Clara shook her head as the girls burst into giggles, but she was smiling, too. She was just trying to hide it from him.

"What's going on in here?"

He hadn't realized Mom had followed him into the kitchen.

"*Onkle* Henwy!" Maggie shrieked this time.

He moved farther into the room, closing in on Clara at the sink. He needed to wash the excess powdered sugar from his fingers and she was standing near.

He tugged on the edge of her apron as Mom said something to the girls behind him.

"You rescued me," he said quietly. Not only the dessert. Clara had called for him at just the right moment, when he needed an escape.

Maybe he could sit through lunch after all—as long as no one talked about Dad's business.

He'd park himself as close to the girls as he could. They made for a great distraction.

"We're ready to eat," Lena called out from the other room.

Henry held out his hand, gratified when Clara slipped her hand in his.

He got caught in her eyes a little, until Mindy's chatter interrupted the moment.

When he turned to go back into the lion's den of the living room, Mom was still standing there. And her eyes had locked on to where he held Clara's hand.

He thought for a minute she was going to say something, but she didn't.

Not until he passed her close to the dining table. She patted his shoulder and whispered, "Hickory Harbor has been good for you."

Clara had ended up seated in the middle of the table, with Henry on one side and Lena on the other.

Whatever had been haunting Henry when he'd walked inside the kitchen, it was gone now. He'd seated himself at the end of the eight-person table, with Mindy directly across from him and Maggie next to her. Henry's parents sat across from each other at the opposite end of the table from Henry.

Todd blessed the food and everyone dug in.

Henry seemed to be engrossed in conversation with Mindy about her new baby brother.

"Are you excited about the tournament?" Lena asked Clara.

Clara swallowed the bite she'd been chewing. "I don't know. Nervous, I guess."

Lena wrinkled her nose. "You shouldn't be. You're far more athletic than I am."

She shook her head. "I don't know why. I've never played before."

"Maybe it was all the farm work while you were growing up," Lena suggested.

"Did you grow up on a farm, dear?" Henry's mother, Kimberly, asked.

Clara had just put a bite in her mouth. At the attention from Henry's mother, her cheeks blazed and she almost choked on her food.

"She did," Lena said. Clara was grateful for her friend as she was able to chew and swallow while Lena explained that she'd grown up with her grandparents on an *Englisher* farm before they'd passed away.

"Why don't you go into business for yourself?" Todd's voice carried to Clara's ears as Lena finished her explanation.

Henry shifted in his seat beside her. His knee pressed into hers beneath the table. "That's not the point," he muttered.

"Did your grandmother teach you to bake? Both the boys have raved about your cookies."

Clara lost the thread of Henry and Todd's conversation as Kimberly engaged her.

"I suppose you would say I taught myself," she said. "My grandmother didn't like cooking much and would insist that cooking breakfast and dinner was enough. But my grandfather had a sweet tooth. I must've been nine or so and found a dessert cookbook at the local library, and once I had permission to try, I made my first batch of cookies."

Henry leaned his elbow on the table and his shoulder into hers. She hadn't even realized he'd been listening. "I think she should write her own cookbook. Every dessert she bakes is delicious."

Clara's face blazed hotter.

Kimberly's eyes lit up. "What a lovely idea."

"I couldn't do that," Clara said quickly. "Baking is just something I do for myself."

Lena looked interested. "I'd buy your cookbook."

"I'd love to have one of your recipes," Kimberly said.

"I'll—I'll write one down for you," Clara said. "You don't need to buy anything."

"You're embarrassing the girl," Henry's father said. He'd been quiet up until now, and at his words, she wanted to sink beneath the table and disappear.

Why had Henry brought up her baking?

Before her thoughts could spiral, Lena leaned over to her. "I've been thinking of bringing on someone to help with some of the cleaning tasks at the center a couple of days a week. Is that something you'd be interested in?"

Clara felt a beat of relief for the change in conversation. She promised to think about it.

As the afternoon wore on, Henry seemed more relaxed, even resting his forearm across the back of Clara's chair as he sprawled in his own.

Conversation turned to David and Ruby and their new baby, and then soon enough, the meal was finished.

When the girls demanded attention from their grandparents and the wall phone rang with a call for the doctor, Clara escaped to the kitchen under the guise of doing dishes.

She just needed a minute.

Henry found her there only moments later, laden down with both hands full of dirty plates.

"You okay?"

She nodded but wrapped her arms around her middle as she looked out the window onto Todd and Lena's backyard.

"My family can be a bit much." There was something in his voice, a tension she didn't recognize.

"It's obvious how much they love you. All of you."

Henry scoffed as he set the plates on the counter and began running water into the sink. "I guess."

"I know you and your father aren't seeing eye to eye right now, but it's obvious how proud he is of you."

Maybe it was the wrong thing to say. A muscle in his jaw clenched.

She wanted to soothe whatever wound was behind that tight expression on his face.

"Sometimes I wish I had one more day with my parents. Or a decade." Or more.

Henry's eyes softened. "I…wondered. When you talk about your grandparents, you didn't seem close to them."

"They did love me, but it wasn't the same."

"No, I guess it wouldn't be."

Clara didn't want him to think she'd had a horrible childhood. That wasn't the truth. "They did the best they could…"

He must've heard something in her voice. An old hurt. "But…" he prompted.

She shook her head, but somehow, after seeing the closeness of his family, she found herself saying, "It wasn't one big thing. It was a thousand little ones. Like when I was in high school and got invited to a birthday party for—an acquaintance, I guess."

Henry made it easier for her to talk by focusing on the dishes, not looking directly at her.

"My grandmother drove me and dropped me off. I walked in and it only took a few seconds to see that I was completely out of place in my handsewn dress and hand-me-down shoes."

She'd spent a long time in the bathroom before the party, doing an elaborate French braid.

All the other girls had worn their hair down with the ends curled. They'd had faces full of makeup.

Clara didn't even own a blusher.

She'd looked over her shoulder from the doorway but Grandma was already halfway down the block. Clara had no choice but to go inside.

She'd spent half the time hiding in a corner, talking to no one. And the rest of the time picking up after the teens who didn't seem to care that their half-filled soda cups were easy to spill.

"It wasn't the party itself," Clara said now. "It was later that night. I cried myself to sleep."

She hadn't had the heart to tell Grandma how awful it had been.

"My mom would've known the moment I got into the car after the party," she said, her thoughts in the past. "She always knew when something was wrong. We had a special bond."

Henry was drying his hands on a towel but it was only a moment before he reached for her.

His embrace offered her comfort, healing she'd longed for.

Clara clung to him, even though she knew she shouldn't. She shouldn't want his hugs.

Shouldn't want his kiss, but she hadn't been able to stop thinking about it since the other night.

"You are blessed to have parents who care about you," she said into his shoulder.

He harrumphed a little laugh.

And then leaned back so she could see his face. Henry's hand cupped her cheek.

"I know why we shouldn't," he said. He was so close. "I'm leaving town in a few weeks. You want someone else."

Henry groaned a little, low in his throat. "But I want this to be real."

When he dipped his head, she was ready for his kiss. She raised up on tiptoe to meet it.

His lips were warm and firm, his touch gentle but just a hint possessive.

Tiny voices from the other room had him backing away from her with a chuckle. He shook his head slightly. "What am I going to do with you?"

Chapter Thirteen

Henry picked up Clara and her bike a couple of days later to go for another practice ride. At midmorning on a sunny fall day, the park was busier.

As they walked together from his truck in the parking lot to the paved trail, she pushed the bike between them. Clara looked nervous.

She also looked beautiful.

Henry noticed that even through his pounding headache. He'd stayed up far too late last night working on the house. He hadn't been able to save the floorboards where paint had soaked in and had had to pull them out one by one and replace them. Then as he had been packing up his truck to leave—long after dark—he'd caught sight of the damaged front door. He'd decided to sand down the door and it had taken much longer than he'd anticipated.

The deadline in three weeks was looming over him and he was beginning to feel as though he couldn't breathe.

And this morning, he'd picked up the phone expecting a mutual friend and gotten Nell.

His ex had talked their mutual friend into letting her use his phone to reach Henry. He never would've answered if he'd known Nell was on the other end. After Henry had given her a terse, chilly dismissal, his friend had texted and apologized for letting Nell use his phone.

Hearing her voice had reopened old wounds. Reminded him of how easy she'd found it to move on from him while they'd still been together. He hadn't been enough for her.

"Is everything all right?" Clara asked now, startling him out of the spiral of thoughts that weren't doing anyone any good.

"Yeah. Of course." Clara didn't need to know about his worries for the house, for his future.

But when she tipped her head and pinned him with that intent stare, he felt as if she could see right through him.

He smiled softly at her. "You want to give this a try?"

She exhaled loudly. "No."

Clara laughed a bit when he raised one eyebrow at her. "Fine."

She moved to straddle the bike. "I can't believe I let you talk me into this again."

"You're going to get it this time." Henry was confident she could do it. "Just think how much more independence you'll have when you can ride all over town instead of walk."

She sighed, but a determined look pressed her lips together.

Clara kicked the bike into motion but only went a few feet before she wobbled erratically and planted her feet back on the ground.

"Good," he said, but she shot him a look that said she knew it was anything but good. "Let me help balance you a bit this time. So you can feel what it's supposed to be like."

Henry held the handlebars and kept pace beside her, but she didn't go any farther than the first time.

This time, her breathing was slightly ragged and he caught a glimpse of her wide eyes.

"Don't be afraid of falling," he said. "I won't let you fall."

Her chin tipped and he followed her gaze to a second parking area across the way. There were two food trucks parked there and several families had gathered. He saw folks in Amish dress, a group of men and women with a couple of little kids running around.

Henry's head was pounding and he felt the tiniest flare of impatience. He planned to get back to work when they finished here. Needed to see it through. And Clara was so close. What was she so afraid of?

"You ready?"

She put her right foot on the pedal at his prompting and they did the same routine again. This time, she lost her balance completely. He kept her elbow and she planted one foot on the ground as the bike crashed to the ground.

"I'm okay," she said.

"I know." The words slipped free, and maybe she sensed the hint of impatience Henry felt because he saw the light in her eyes dim. She pulled away from his touch and averted her face as she bent to pick up the bike.

"I can hear your stomach rumbling," she said. "Maybe we should stop for a while and you can grab something to eat."

Henry thought of the unfinished bedroom floor and his instinct was to say no. He had work to do. And they'd barely gotten started with the bike.

But Clara's hands were trembling and she was looking toward the group of folks now hovering on the grassy area near some picnic tables not far away. If she was distracted, this wasn't going to work.

And he was hungry. Maybe some food would settle him.

Henry gave in and she pushed the bike over to one of the picnic tables as he ordered for both of them from one of the food trucks.

By the time he joined her at the table, the group of friends had come over.

He recognized Abe's brother and two girls from their volleyball team, Samantha and Trudy. He was introduced to Robert and Penny and sat down the paper containers of food to shake hands with them.

Clara was clearly embarrassed when Trudy motioned to the bike she'd propped against the other side of the big concrete picnic table.

"Are you learning to ride?"

"No," Clara mumbled.

Henry gave an exasperated sigh. "Yes, she is."

"I'm not any good at it," Clara argued, her eyes sparking at him.

Samantha leaned in. "I think it's impressive that you're trying. I never could learn how to sew a straight line. My mother tried to teach me over and over when I was younger—she even got my *grossmammi* and *aendis* to give me lessons. I still can't."

The other girls giggled and Clara joined in hesitantly with raised brows. "Really?"

"It's true," Trudy said.

And then Micah chimed in. "Our horses hate me," he admitted cheerfully. "I've never had the knack with them."

Clara seemed stunned by this information that other people weren't perfect and had things they considered faults.

"You're the one remodeling the house on County Road 67, aren't you?" Robert asked Henry.

"That's right."

"My house is another mile up the road."

Henry grimaced. "I hope I haven't kept you up nights with my power tools."

The other man grinned. "Not that I've heard." He glanced

between Henry and Clara. "Too much time courting to get your work in during the daytime hours?"

"I wish." Henry mentioned the break-in and second vandalism, careful to turn his body away, aware that Clara was still in conversation with her friends.

She'd lit up now as he caught a few words about snacks for the tournament.

Clara's eyes were alight and she was smiling, joining in the conversation. Gone was the girl who'd been nervous to get out of his truck that first night at volleyball practice.

It hit him hard. This was where Clara belonged. She was the perfect fit for Hickory Harbor. The local young people just hadn't known it. He had no doubt these young ladies would discover what an amazing person she was and fast friendships would form.

And then where would Henry be?

Gone. Back to his life in Columbus.

The thought made his appetite disappear.

"Ah."

He was knocked out of his thoughts when he realized Robert had been talking to him.

"Sorry."

Robert grinned. "I can understand the distraction."

What did that mean? That he thought Clara was just as lovely as Henry did?

"I was saying that I'd be happy to keep an eye on your place. There are two families closer and I'm sure they wouldn't mind keeping an eye out, either. You can't be home all the time."

"You'd do that?"

Robert shrugged. "Of course."

The strangeness of it wasn't lost on Henry. This wasn't some big city where neighbors didn't know each other's names.

And Robert was offering to let him be a part of the community.

"Uh, thanks." Henry couldn't afford another setback.

Micah edged closer and popped one eyebrow. "So you and Clara are serious, huh?"

Henry glanced back to see Clara with her head bent over a book one of the young ladies had pulled from a backpack.

His chest felt tight and achy. She'd told him from the start that she wanted an Amish husband. He wasn't that.

"No," he said quietly. "We're not serious."

No. We're not serious.

Henry's words bounced around Clara's brain as her friends took their leave.

She wasn't meant to have heard them. Henry had been speaking softly and half turned away from her conversation with the others.

But now the words were burned into her brain.

Henry was quiet and thoughtful as they ate the tacos he'd bought from one of the trucks.

Clara didn't taste any of it and mostly pushed it around her plate.

The last time they'd been together, he'd kissed her and held her tenderly and she'd thought…

She'd forgotten that he'd only wanted his mother to believe they were together.

"It's not as good as yours."

Henry's words didn't register at first. He repeated them, waving the cookie he'd taken one bite out of before he set it back in the paper container in front of him.

The confusion swirling around in her gut made her blurt, "Why did you say that? To your mom."

He looked confused.

"At lunch last Wednesday, you told her I should write a cookbook."

"You should." He took a sip of the soda from the paper cup. "Or open a bakery. That would be even better."

She shook her head. "Hickory Harbor already has an Amish bakery."

His intent stare landed on her. "Your desserts are better."

For one moment, Clara felt a stirring of pride. He thought her desserts were better than an established bakery's?

And then he spoke again. "I don't get why you hide your talent."

"I don't."

His chin jutted. "Then why don't you write that cookbook? You can't be happy cleaning houses. Where is the future in that?"

Her stomach twisted. Why was Henry pushing?

The truth was, Clara hadn't been happy living in Dorcas's house for a long time. But she'd never considered her baking as an option for work. It was only a hobby.

"If you're scared nobody would buy your cookbook, you don't need to be. I think my mom would buy a hundred copies herself and hand them out to all her friends."

Henry didn't understand. "That's not it. I share my baking. I bring my desserts to Sunday meals."

He shook his head. "And no one knows that they are yours."

That didn't matter. "Pride is a sin," she said.

"I'm not talking about that." He rubbed his hands down his face. Clara heard his sigh. Maybe he wasn't trying to hide it.

Henry stood up. "I'm going to wash up." He motioned to the public bathrooms before he scooped up their trash.

He left his phone on the table.

Clara felt confused and heavy inside. She wished she'd stayed home this morning. She glared at the bike. She hadn't wanted to disappoint Henry. That's why she said yes. She wished she'd never seen that bike.

Independence. Is that what Henry wanted for her? After he left Hickory Harbor?

She swallowed hard.

Henry's phone chimed and she shouldn't have looked but a box with the name Nell popped up. Clara found herself leaning in and squinting at the tiny picture on the screen.

This was Nell?

She was beautiful, with long blond hair cascading down her back. The tiny photo didn't reveal what color her eyes were, but her features were elfin and perfect.

This was the kind of woman Henry had dated before. Been engaged to.

Someone beautiful and sophisticated. No doubt Nell had an important career and dozens of friends.

If the two of them had been put side by side, Clara wouldn't compare.

Nell had broken Henry's heart, Clara reminded herself. He didn't love Nell anymore.

But he had once.

Clara didn't know what to say when he returned, only that she felt as shy and wrong-footed as she had in the very beginning.

Dorcas's biting words from weeks ago crashed through her mind.

But her great-aunt had been worried for the wrong reasons. Henry wasn't going to turn her into an *Englisher*. He'd made no mention of their relationship lasting longer than his time in Hickory Harbor.

And she wanted to be with him. In a real relationship.

Henry squinted in the sunlight. "Do you want to try the bike again?"

She swallowed hard. "Not today." She stood up and took the bike from where it'd been propped against the table. "I think I'd better get home. My aunt might need help with chores."

Henry considered her for a long moment that stretched. Until Clara looked down at the bike as she began to roll it back down the path toward his truck.

"I could come in and help. Meet your great-aunt."

She choked back a shocked laugh. She was sure that would be a disaster. She could only imagine the cruel words Dorcas might hurl at Henry.

"I don't think that's a good idea."

Clara guided the bike around a bumpy pothole in the paved path, and when she glanced up, she saw a flash of emotion on his face before it went carefully blank.

It was only a few more moments before they reached his truck and he opened the tailgate. He moved to take the handlebars from her and they came face-to-face. She couldn't help noticing the determined set of his jaw.

"Look, I'm sorry if I hurt your feelings earlier." Henry hefted the bike into the truck bed and then turned back to her. "It kills me to see you hide yourself away."

His words made her stomach drop. She wrapped her arms around her middle. "I don't—"

"Yes, you do. You keep quiet and hold back what you really want or need because you think it's too much trouble for the people around you."

Clara shook her head, denying his words. Even as they speared like an arrow straight in her heart.

"You're more than you give yourself credit for. You're a good friend. A good niece. An incredible baker."

There was a hot prickling behind her nose.

Clara couldn't help picturing the beautiful *Englisher* Nell. She tried to hide the tremble of her lip by biting it. She kept her eyes wide and stared off into the distance, doing her best to keep tears at bay.

Henry made a noisy sigh of dissatisfaction.

"Now you've gone all silent on me."

She flared her nostrils against the urge to let tears fall and looked right at him. "I'm not the only one hiding," she said. Her emotion pushed the words out, made them sound stronger than she felt. "You haven't told your father how much you've been working on this house. You haven't asked for help. You're not being truthful with him and it's no wonder he is selling the business."

She gasped as the words left her mouth.

Henry flinched.

"I—I'm sorry. I didn't mean—"

He closed his eyes and then opened them again. Ran a hand through his hair. When he looked at her, she saw only a carefully blank expression. "I think we've forgotten what we're doing here. We started out with a plan, but things have gotten muddy. Maybe we need to step back. Stick with the original plan."

Clara felt a new rush of tears as his meaning sank in. Stick to pretend dating.

She couldn't say a word or she'd start crying. So she only nodded and got in the truck.

Chapter Fourteen

"Where is Clara?" Todd asked.

Henry glanced at his brother and down at the sneaker he was tying. "I don't know."

The brothers stood in a grassy area in a big open field that Henry hadn't realized was part of the local park. Ten different volleyball courts had been set up, with official-sized nets and sidelines staked out in the grass that had been mowed short. There were portable bleachers that had been set up alongside the courts on either end, and families and spectators were spread out in camp chairs and picnic blankets.

There were people everywhere, all of them dressed in the Amish way, with long pants and suspenders for the men, over their button-up shirts. The women wore dresses and tennis shoes and looked ready to play.

Where *was* Clara?

"She wasn't at home when I stopped by to pick her up. The house seemed empty," he explained.

Todd's forehead wrinkled. "Do you think she's all right?"

Henry shrugged. He was trying not to worry.

It had been almost a week since Henry had seen her. He missed her.

The practice on Tuesday night had been canceled due to rainstorms and Henry had skipped the Thursday evening practice to finish staining the wood floor in the bedroom. He'd phoned Todd at the clinic that day and asked his brother and Lena to pick up Clara and bring her to Thursday's practice, and to give his apologies.

Clara hadn't been at Sunday house church, either.

Henry didn't like the way things had ended last Saturday, the tense silence between them. Looking back, he knew he hadn't been at his best.

He just needed to get out from under the house. If Dad would give him a chance, he knew he could prove himself.

"She's not in the restrooms and I didn't see her near the parking area." Lena sounded a little out of breath as she joined them.

Behind Lena, Samuel looked up from a clipboard he was holding. He had a bag full of volleyballs at his feet. "I can't register our team without all members present. And we've only got a few minutes left…"

Henry had already tucked his truck keys in the gym bag he'd brought with him. "Do you think I should go back to her house?"

Todd considered for a moment. "You know her better than anyone else."

But he must've seen something in Henry's expression, because he sidled closer.

"What's going on? Did you break up?"

"No." Henry didn't mean to say the word with that much force behind it, but the idea of not seeing Clara again was like a giant fist squeezing his lungs. "Things have… We had a disagreement last weekend and I haven't been able to talk to her."

"Why not?"

"Because I've been busy trying to meet the deadline for Dad's house!" The words exploded out of him, though he spoke at a low volume.

Todd knew him. Maybe too well. He frowned. "You're behind schedule?"

Henry didn't have to nod.

"Why didn't you say something?"

"Why would I?" Henry didn't try to hide the touch of bitterness in his voice. "You've got this great new life. A new job, community. And Lena."

"I have time for you."

Todd being here was part of the reason Henry had said yes to a project in Hickory Harbor. He'd hoped to recapture some of the closeness he and Todd had lost after his brother had left for college.

"If you need help," Todd said, "you have to ask—"

"Sorry I'm late." Clara's embarrassed murmur was barely out before there were exclamations of her name.

Lena threw her arms around Clara's shoulders.

Henry met her gaze over Lena's shoulder and saw that her cheeks were pink—not from embarrassment but from exertion. She was breathing hard, like she'd run a long distance.

Henry bent to pull one of the water bottles out of his bag. Lena let Clara go and Samuel left to file their team paperwork.

Clara accepted greetings from their teammates but seemed grateful when Henry guided her a few steps away and pressed the water bottle into her hands.

"Thanks," she said. "I—I forgot my bag."

"I brought extra to share. What happened? I went by your house…"

She was frazzled, pushing hair behind her ears that had come loose and curled around her temple. She didn't quite meet his eye. "Dorcas didn't want me to play."

The team started doing exercises designed to warm up their muscles. Henry and Clara joined the end of the line as each person walked with high knees and swung their arms side to side.

Henry was aware of Todd shooting looks at him. Henry didn't kid himself that their conversation was over. He should probably ask Todd not to say anything to Dad.

"What do you mean?" he asked Clara. "I thought your aunt was fine with you playing on an Amish team."

Her lips pressed together and she shook her head slightly, averting her face when they reached the end of an invisible line and turned around to do lunges as they walked the opposite direction. At any other time, Henry would've gotten a kick out of seeing people dressed in jeans or slacks and long dresses doing these exercises that he'd only seen people in sports uniforms complete. It was a little mind-blowing.

But he was concerned about Clara.

"She just…didn't want me to come. I was at my cousin's house and decided to walk over."

There was more Clara wasn't telling him. He could see it in the way her eyes darted away from his.

"Did you tell her you were coming?"

She shook her head, guilt written clearly on her face. "I already know what you're going to say," she whispered fiercely. "That I should stand up for myself." Her eyes had grown bright and shone with tears, and he wanted nothing more than to find a private place and pull her into his arms.

"You don't understand what it's like," she said, still in that fierce whisper. "I don't have anyone else. There's no other home for me to go to."

I don't have anyone else.

The words hit him in the soft underbelly. Henry ached for her. "You might not think so, but I understand."

The team broke into smaller groups and it allowed them

to pair off and move several steps away as they bounced a ball between them off the low grass.

Henry kept his voice low to keep from being overheard. "Todd was too busy for me once he hit med school. And when things started going south with Nell, my parents had just found out about David. Everything changed. I couldn't drag myself to work. My dad didn't even notice because he'd pulled back from the job we'd been working on together. When I spoke to my mom and tried to tell her what was going on, she was distracted and distant. I had no one to turn to…"

And about then was when Nell's manipulative behavior had begun, making the situation ten times worse.

He shoved thoughts of his ex away. "I get it, because I've been through it. I messed up the big contracting job and that's why I have to prove myself now—but that's not what I want you—"

"We're playing our first game on field eight!" Samuel's voice rang out, interrupting Henry.

Clara's tears had dried up and maybe that was enough for now. The team was grabbing belongings and preparing to move across to another court on the opposite side of the gathering.

He hadn't meant to go into such a long explanation.

What he'd wanted to say was, *You're not alone. You've got me.*

You might not think so, but I understand.

Clara stood on the sidelines as her team played the second set of their first game. She had started the first set but hadn't touched the ball before she'd rotated off and had to wait to go back in.

That was just fine with her.

She hadn't anticipated how nervous she would feel on the grassy court.

And she was still completely unsettled from this morning.

Dorcas had surprised her in the kitchen when she'd been standing at the counter eating a quick breakfast of scrambled eggs and toast.

"I refuse to let you see that *Englisher* again."

Those words had settled like a stone in her gut.

"I made a commitment to my team. The tournament is all day."

"I told your cousin you would come and help her can pumpkins today."

"But you knew about the tournament."

Clara's argument hadn't mattered. Dorcas had been determined and Clara had been shaken by the time Emily had arrived in a buggy.

The entire ride to her cousin's house, Clara had fought off tears. When Emily had asked why she was so quiet and Clara had told her about Dorcas's demand, Emily's response had been, *Maybe she's right.*

Clara had worked up the courage to walk to the fields, though she knew Dorcas would be angry. Clara would beg for forgiveness later.

The agreement between Clara and Henry had an end date. He was leaving town in another two weeks.

Maybe it was time to end this pretense. No more pretending. No more lessons.

At the very least, Clara had made a commitment to Todd and Lena and the rest of their team. She wouldn't shirk it. Surely Dorcas would understand that.

But her stomach still felt twisted and her palms sweaty as she waited to go back into the game.

"Are you all right?" Lena whispered from her place beside Clara. "You look like you aren't feeling well."

"I'm just nervous. I don't want to make a mistake."

Clara caught Henry's eye as the rotation changed. He stood opposite her on the court. He flashed her a smile but all she could think about was him saying that his family had all but abandoned him.

"Clara, you're in next."

Don't sub me in. But the words caught in her throat. She couldn't do this.

The score was tied but the other team made the next point and then Samuel was waving her in.

Clara wanted to run back out of the court. Run all the way back to her cousin's house and claim this was a mistake.

Her heart pounded and she could only hear the voices of her teammates calling encouragement as if from a distance. Her mouth was dry and jitters went up and down her spine.

Don't let the ball come to me.

But the opposite happened. An easy ball came over the net and she reached for it...and missed. Clara watched in horror as it touched the ground near her feet.

"I'm sorry." She didn't know whether she mouthed the words or said them.

The other team took a second serve and this time Trudy hit a hard ball across the net and scored a point.

And Samuel was pointing her to the server's position.

Clara shook her head, but he smiled patiently. "It's your serve."

She didn't have a choice. She had to do it.

Clara heard a quiet, "You can do this," from Todd, who was in the position next to her.

She bounced the ball on the grass once. It felt off the moment she balanced it in her hand.

Clara's serve hit the net and bounced back on their team's side.

She'd lost another point for their team.

There was a roaring in her ears and her face felt hot.

Clara heard the cadence of Henry calling out to her from the sideline, but she couldn't make out his words.

The team didn't recover, losing several more points before the referee called the match.

She joined the team for a few encouraging words from their coach. They'd have a short break and then play another match.

The huddle broke up and all Clara wanted was escape from her confusing feelings, her guilt over practically losing the match for her team.

But Henry followed her as she scurried toward the restrooms across the grassy field.

"I need a minute," she called over her shoulder to him.

"Hang on a sec—"

She didn't want to.

But Henry grasped her arm and wouldn't let go. She turned to face him, realizing they were standing beneath a tall oak, separated from the crowd and players in a semiprivate area.

"I never should have played." She cast her eyes to the ground.

"That wasn't your fault." His voice was soft and kind. "Volleyball is a team sport."

"And it's more than obvious that I shouldn't be on the team." She was terrible.

"Nobody on the team cares that you had an off game. I've seen you in practice and you're better than what just happened."

Clara could still feel the tension between them. She hadn't spoken to him in almost a week and she'd felt the desperation of knowing their friendship was almost at its end.

All of it bubbled up inside her.

I don't want us to end. But the words were stuck in her throat.

He'd once accused her of hiding her true self.

Maybe he was right.

But it felt too frightening to tell him that truth.

"I'll be back in a minute," she murmured, trying to pull away.

"Clara." The urgency and serious tone in his voice stopped her.

She swallowed hard, still unable to look at him.

"Before the game, what I was trying to tell you was this." Henry tipped her chin up with his knuckle.

The tenderness in his gaze took her breath away. It made a raw and scary hope take root.

"You are not alone." He said the words as if he was imparting a state secret. "You have me."

Clara swallowed back the hot knot of emotion clogging her throat. "But—you said—"

He brushed her jaw with his thumb. "I know what I said. I messed up."

The hope inside her took flight. "You—you did?"

He nodded and his hand fell away. "There's something real between us. I want—"

Clara didn't need to hear any more. Not at this moment. She stretched up on tiptoe and reached for him, brushing a kiss across his lips.

When she backed away—quickly, because there were people all around—his eyes were dancing.

"Okay. We'll talk more later?"

She nodded. Her heart was suddenly so light.

And when they walked back to the court to join the team to strategize for the next game, he held her hand.

Chapter Fifteen

After winning two games, the team's spirits were high.

Clara felt as if she was floating on air.

But not because she'd returned several balls over the net and even served an unhittable ball.

She felt as light as a helium-filled balloon because of the way Henry's eyes lit up when their gazes collided. The way his hand had brushed hers when they'd passed each other subbing in and out of the game. The knowledge that he was driving her home tonight and she would receive another one of his kisses.

Their team had a scheduled lunch break and moved away from the activity at the courts and to a roped-off area reserved for teams.

Samantha spread two picnic blankets while Lena and Trudy unloaded sack lunches from a cooler. Todd and Henry handed out bottles of electrolyte drinks and water.

Clara accepted the gentle teasing when Trudy said, "I was hoping you'd bring some of your macadamia nut cookies."

Samuel chimed in with, "I think we all were."

Clara felt a flush of pleasure.

Henry took a seat kitty-corner to her on the picnic blanket and accepted one of the sack lunches from Lena.

"I've been thinking of writing a recipe book," Clara said shyly.

She barely heard the chorus of excitement and well wishes from the friends around her because she was caught in Henry's stare. He raised one expressive eyebrow. "You are?"

"I thought about what you said. A lot. I've already started writing the recipes."

She watched the warmth grow in his eyes.

The conversation moved on and she took a few minutes to eat quietly.

Even though Clara had balked at his suggestion that she make her baking into something profitable, she hadn't been able to get it out of her mind.

Henry believed in her.

And it seemed her friends did, too.

As Henry finished eating, he scooted into a vacant seat next to her and leaned back on his palms. His shoulder leaned against hers. He took some teasing from his brother on a serve Henry had missed.

Clara noticed Lena observing just how close she and Henry were sitting. It shouldn't matter. But Lena had become a friend. And she was Henry's sister-in-law. Clara wanted her friend to approve.

"Did you finish painting?" Robert asked Henry.

They were sitting close enough that Clara felt the tension grab him.

She looked at him questioningly.

Henry was smiling, but she saw the way it didn't quite meet his eyes. "I haven't gotten to the painting yet."

"More delays?" Todd asked.

If anything, his question made Henry's tension ratchet up. Henry sat up, brushing off his hands.

Clara felt the absence of his warmth at her side.

"Everything's fine," he said. "Just taking longer than expected. Par for the course on this job."

"My brothers and I could come over after work on Monday," Samuel offered. "We aren't master builders, but we can wield a paintbrush at least."

Trudy offered, "I could help, too."

Henry laughed a little. "Guys, I'm fine. The work will get done."

But Clara saw the way his knuckles were still white against the tan of his skin.

She found herself nudging Henry's thigh with her knee. When he looked at her, she said, "You should say yes. Let your friends help. You don't have to do it by yourself."

You're not alone.

He seemed to understand the words she didn't say and she saw the softening in his expression. "I'll think about it."

Henry glanced at his watch. "Next match will be here before we know it. I've got another cooler in the truck with more water. I'll go get it."

The rest of the group began picking up their things when they were joined by the other Hickory Harbor team. Abe's team.

There was some friendly ribbing between the two teams and Clara found herself smiling as she folded the picnic blanket she'd sat on.

"Need some help?" Abe asked. If Clara was surprised by his question, she was more so by the intent way he watched her and how close he stood.

"I think I've got it." She made a fold where she could hug the blanket in front of her.

"I watched you playing earlier."

Clara didn't know what to say to that. Did he mean he'd

watched their team? It sounded as if he'd said he was watching her, but that couldn't be what he'd meant. Could it?

"You had some good hits."

Abe's compliment made her blush. He had meant he'd been watching her. Why?

"Oh. Thank you."

There was color high on his cheeks. The way he was looking at her made her heart pound.

Was he...noticing her? Finally?

She'd agreed to Henry's dating plan for this very reason, but as she stood near Abe, feeling more bashful than ever, she couldn't help thinking that something was missing.

Abe cleared his throat. "I never realized... I mean—" He cut himself off and rubbed one hand on the back of his neck.

His uncertainty made her discomfort multiply.

"Would you go to the singing with me next week?"

Clara's breath caught in her chest.

No.

Her brain supplied an instant refusal. The only person she wanted to attend a singing with was Henry.

But before Clara could say a word, she registered someone coming alongside her. Dorcas leaning on her walking cane.

Shock rendered Clara immobile as her great-aunt smiled at Abe. "Of course she will."

No.

For the second time, the word wouldn't pass her lips.

"*Goot.* Okay. I'll, uh...see you later."

Abe joined his team as they moved off, sending one more look over his shoulder at her.

Clara was left with Dorcas.

"What are you doing here?"

Dorcas's mouth was twisted in a frown but her eyes were

calculating. "Your cousin came back to tell me you'd abandoned her. She drove me here."

That still didn't explain what Dorcas was doing here, meddling in Clara's decisions.

"Why did you tell him that I would—" Clara shook her head, still reeling.

"You cannot take up with that *Englisher* boy. Don't make the mistake your mother did when she ran away with your father." Dorcas's voice twisted when she said the last words, like she still hated Clara's father.

"I—" The words were right there, to tell Dorcas that she wouldn't go to the singing with Abe, that Clara wanted Henry.

But Dorcas was smiling at her. "You tried to tell me. That this volleyball would provide an opportunity for you to find an Amish husband."

Clara felt frozen.

Her great-aunt was happy.

The very thing she'd wanted in the beginning had happened. For Abe to notice her, for him to invite her... This might even be considered the beginning of a courtship.

But Clara felt at war with herself.

Her heart wanted Henry. He was the one who encouraged her to be herself.

And still, she felt the draw of Dorcas's approval. She couldn't force the words out to argue with her.

Clara felt panicked and sick inside.

Dorcas didn't seem to notice. She patted Clara's arm—the first time she'd initiated contact. "I'll stay and watch your next game. Is there a place I can sit?" Clara felt conspicuous, like everyone was watching her. Where was Henry?

If he'd been near, maybe Clara would've had the strength to refuse.

But she looked around and didn't see him among the spectators or players nearby.

She fought against the building knot in her gut as she followed her aunt across the grounds.

Henry felt numb and had to look down at his hands where he clutched the cooler to make sure he was still holding on to it.

Would you go to the singing with me next week?

Of course she will.

Oh, he shouldn't have eavesdropped. He had been headed back to where Clara was, when he'd seen her holding her picnic blanket while she talked to Abe. Henry had held back when it became obvious that the other man was trying to express his interest in Clara.

What had Henry thought? That Clara was going to say no?

That Henry mattered so much to her she'd go against her aunt?

Henry was the one who'd made a declaration today. He had told Clara that she wasn't alone. He only realized now that she had hinted at the same for him when they'd been conversing with the group, but she hadn't outright said the same thing back.

He couldn't face her right now, not when he felt so unmoored and hurt.

But Henry also couldn't let his team down and they were scheduled to play next.

He kept his head down while Samuel gave an inspiring pep talk on the sidelines of the court.

With his eyes downcast, all Henry saw was Clara's expression when she had been talking to her aunt. She hadn't been arguing with her aunt, that was for sure. Her expression had been filled with hope.

Henry should've told Samuel he needed a minute to gather himself, but he was put in on the first rotation and started playing horribly. He missed two balls off the bat and made several bobbles that his team had to save.

He couldn't meet Clara's eyes. What was he supposed to say if she told him she was courting with Abe?

Relief flowed when he was out for a rotation. Henry stood on the sideline, rubbing his shoulder. His brain presented him a picture of Clara as she had appeared that morning. She'd been deeply shaken at the idea of upsetting her great-aunt. *She's the only family I have.*

The relationship Clara and Henry had was vague and undefined. They'd started out pretending.

But he'd fallen for her, wanted to make their relationship real. With all these thoughts swirling in his head, he couldn't remember if she'd ever said she'd wanted things to be real. Had Clara just gone along with him, humored him this entire time?

No. When she'd kissed him, that was real.

But had he thought things through? Past the end date of Dad's build?

Henry hadn't seriously thought about staying in Hickory Harbor. Hadn't thought about what that would mean for a relationship.

Was he prepared to ask Clara to give up the life she'd chosen here? She told him why she had joined the Amish church, told him about the community that she had hoped to find.

On the court, he saw Samantha give Clara a high five in between points.

Clara had found what she'd been looking for, hadn't she? Acceptance with the small group of players. Friendships growing. And she had a man who wanted to come courting.

With Clara's sweet spirit and kindness, it wouldn't be long before everyone realized how wonderful she was. And if Abe wasn't smart enough to snatch her up, some other man would be. An Amish man, who would keep her integrated into this community.

Henry felt sick to his stomach.

And then Todd was nudging him as they switched places, and Henry went in for the next rotation.

"Get your head in the game," his brother said.

But it was no use. Henry was pretty much useless, and his team had to compensate for his mental distraction during the second set, which they won.

"Can I talk to you for a minute?"

The game was barely over and Henry hadn't been able to muddle through his thoughts to a solution.

Abe stood in front of him, looking nervous.

Henry used the hem of his T-shirt to wipe sweat from his face. He sighed. "Sure."

The other man shifted from foot to foot. "I spoke to Clara. Asked her to go with me to the singing next week."

Henry wanted to snap at the guy.

But Abe's earnest expression kept him from doing so.

"My brother told me he'd run into you at the park and that he'd asked whether you were serious. About Clara."

Henry watched the guy, certain that if he'd had his hat in hand, he'd be turning it around and around.

Henry wanted to howl at the unfairness of it all. He was serious about Clara. He was falling for her.

Abe wasn't finished. "I think Clara is a fine young woman. Someone…someone worth marrying."

Henry felt like the other man had punched him in the gut. His chest was tight and it was difficult to draw breath.

Henry saw in his mind's eye Clara facing off with her aunt, uncertain and vulnerable.

And then a memory from when they'd first begun their charade. Clara leaning across the restaurant table, her eyes pleading with him to understand as she explained her loneliness, how much she wanted to belong.

Henry glanced down at his clothing. He'd stuck out like a sore thumb today, the only *Englisher* playing in this tournament.

He didn't fit here.

Clara did. And this was what she wanted.

Henry couldn't compete with Abe, couldn't give her the acceptance she wanted.

If he fought for her, if he told Abe that they were serious, how long would it be before she realized that being with Henry was a mistake?

He wasn't staying in Hickory Harbor. It would be much more difficult to see each other with distance between them. It wasn't like he could call her on the phone.

"Clara can make up her own mind," he said, the words cutting his throat like glass.

He could see that it wasn't the cut-and-dry answer that Abe wanted, but it was all Henry could give him right now.

Chapter Sixteen

Monday afternoon, Henry was working through his unresolved feelings by tearing out the tree stump from the middle of the backyard.

It wasn't the finishing work he was supposed to be doing, but he needed the physical labor.

He'd dug around the base of the stump and used a chain saw to cut through sections of the big connecting roots that spread on each side. Now he was using the shovel again, doing his best to dig beneath the base of the stump.

He was dirty and sweaty.

And no closer to sorting through his emotions than when he'd started.

His cell phone rang.

He pushed the shovel into the ground and reached into his pocket with grubby hands to answer it.

Dad.

Great.

"Hey, Dad."

"Henry." There was a muffled sound of a door closing. "Do you have a few minutes to talk?"

"All right." Henry strode back to the porch, where he'd left a jug of water. He'd slake his thirst while he listened.

"I closed the business sale today. Everything is finalized."

Henry had thought he had more time. Thought he was braced for what his dad was going to say, but he felt as if the wind was knocked out of him.

His suddenly nerveless fingers dropped his jug back on the porch with a clank. He sat down heavily.

Dad had told him this was in the works, hadn't he? But up until this moment, he'd held on to a thread of hope.

"Henry, this isn't a reflection of you or the work you've done."

Wasn't it, though? Things might've been different if he'd been able to complete the Dudley house.

He was surprised by the stinging in his eyes and swiped his palm down his face before realizing he'd probably covered himself in mud.

"Henry?"

"I'm happy for you, Dad." It was a fib. He'd find a way to be happy for his parents later. His mom had wanted this for Dad for years. Retirement and time for Dad to slow down.

Henry hadn't expected it to be at his expense.

"Patterson and I are going to work together to close out the jobs that are still open. Don't worry about finishing up on the Hickory Harbor house."

Dad's words flowed over him as he stared at the ground. Something was moving.

Henry let his gaze flick up and saw a orange-and-white kitten with its side against the house, peering around the corner. A gray-and-white kitten was stalking a grasshopper in the long patch of weeds. A third kitten, the calico, slowly crossed the space and bent her head to sniff Henry's boot.

"So you want me to walk away?" His voice scared the kitten and she jumped away.

"Patterson and I will drive out next week and make a list of what his crew needs to do to finish."

That was it, apparently. Henry was done with the house and with Hickory Harbor.

The calico sniffed in his direction once more and then moved off, exploring the same direction her gray brother had gone.

"If you decide not to stay on, you'll get a lump sum," Dad said. "Enough to tide you over until you find something else."

Bitterness rose in his throat.

"Patterson is a good builder. You'd do well leading one of his teams."

Work for the man who'd taken over the business Henry had wanted since he was a boy? He couldn't stomach it.

"Henry?"

"I gotta go. I'll talk to you soon."

Dad was still talking, but Henry hung up. It was rude, not the respect his dad deserved. He'd have to apologize the next time he saw his dad.

Henry's head had started to pound sometime during that call.

He stared sightlessly ahead, until he caught sight of Mama Kitty sitting in the center of the hole underneath the house. She was watching over her babies.

"They're about ready to fly the coop," he said.

She gazed off, pretending she couldn't hear him.

The kittens were big enough to be adopted out.

His dad had made it so he didn't have to finish the house. Henry was done.

There was nothing keeping him in Hickory Harbor.

Except for Clara.

If he tried to make a real relationship work, how long would it take her to figure out that she'd made a mistake?

Dad had.

Todd chose medicine, had left Henry behind.

Nell had known him the best out of everyone, and she'd found him lacking.

Henry was kidding himself if he thought Clara—beautiful, kind, amazing Clara—wouldn't figure out that she was better off without him eventually.

And that might just kill him.

Henry stood up so fast that he startled the kittens, who darted back toward their mom.

He brushed off a bit of the dirt before he got in the truck.

It was only a matter of minutes before he drove up to Clara's farmhouse.

Clara was outside, working in the garden.

He shut off the truck and got out.

"Hi. What are you doing here?"

Henry couldn't tell if it was curiosity or if she was worried about him being here.

"I need to talk to you."

She stood up and he saw she was wearing the same worn dress she'd had on that first day, when she'd come to clean for him. Her apron was dirty in the front, where she'd been kneeling in the garden.

Clara caught him staring and ducked her head, brushing at the dirt on her apron. "Dorcas was clearing out before winter sets in. She thinks she tweaked her back and asked me to clear the rest for her."

That band around his chest tightened and he could barely draw a breath.

What a time to figure out that he wasn't falling in love with her—he already loved her. Even with a streak of dirt across one cheek and wearing her old beat-up dress...there was no hiding her inner beauty.

She glanced toward the house, and he realized she'd done the same when he'd first driven up.

Was Clara worried her aunt would see him out here?

It was a cruel reminder that he was an outsider in Hickory Harbor. His stomach twisted.

"I saw you talking to Abe during the tournament on Saturday."

The smile that had been lingering around her eyes faded.

Henry wouldn't bring up that Abe had approached him after the last game.

Why was this so hard? His throat ached and he worked to keep emotion out of it.

"I think you should be with him." He had to clear his throat before he could get any more words out. Especially when Clara's eyes went luminous.

He soldiered on. "That was our deal from the beginning. You get an Amish husband."

It was what she'd wanted the most.

He just didn't expect it to hurt so much to walk away.

I think you should be with Abe.
I don't want to be with Abe.
The words stuck in Clara's throat.

She'd spent two days trying to figure out how to tell Dorcas that she wasn't going to the singing with Abe. She hadn't even considered how she would get a message to the man himself.

Dorcas had been more talkative, happy with Clara over the past two days.

Maybe that's why Clara hadn't been able to tell her.

Henry was looking off to the side, a muscle jumping in his cheek. He'd told her what he came to say, but maybe there was still a chance—

"I'd rather spend time with you," she said hesitantly. "Before you go back to Columbus."

His chin jutted, showing the tendons in his neck, before he said, "My dad sold the business. I won't finish the house after all."

Oh, Henry.

She knew he must be heartbroken. Henry wanted a chance to prove himself, to convince his father he could run the business.

She started to reach for him, but he stepped back, putting more distance between them.

His eyes met hers, closed off and distant. "It's for the best, right?"

Her heart tripped. "What do you mean?"

"We always knew this thing—" his hand gestured between them "—had an end date. But you got what you wanted. Abe wants to come courting. He told me after the tournament. He could see himself marrying you."

The words that would've been a blessing before she'd met Henry only made her feel as if she couldn't breathe.

I don't want to marry Abe.

Again the words wouldn't come.

"Henry, I—" *am in love with you.*

He'd turned his face away again.

This time Clara realized the back door had slammed.

Numb, she turned to see Dorcas hobbling down the steps and across the grass toward them.

"You aren't welcome here." Dorcas said the hurtful words to Henry, who blinked.

He glanced back to Clara. "I came to say goodbye."

Clara swallowed a hot knot of tears. "What will you do now?"

"That's none of your concern," Dorcas snapped.

Henry didn't look away from Clara. In the depths of his

eyes, she could see his despair. He'd wanted his father's approval. Wanted the business.

"I don't know."

She wanted to reach out to him.

"Clara, come inside."

She wanted to snap at Dorcas. Wanted to ask how she could be so cold. Couldn't Dorcas see that Clara's relationship was ending?

But Clara's vocal chords remained frozen and Henry finally blinked, breaking the stare between them.

"See you around," he muttered.

Wait.

But Dorcas took Clara's arm and urged her toward the house as Henry trudged toward his truck.

"Now that's done," Dorcas said.

Clara pulled her arm away. "That hurts." Dorcas had pinched her, holding on too tightly, but it was her heart in shreds that was the real source of pain.

"You're finally making better choices," Dorcas said. "The singing will be fun. Abe is a *goot* Amish man."

She hadn't made the choice at all, had she? Dorcas had appeared and made it for her.

And now Henry had chosen for her, too.

She hadn't been able to say the words to argue with him. That they should be together.

"I need—"

Clara turned to go after Henry. Maybe it wasn't too late—

But he'd already started the truck and was backing out of the driveway.

"Stop!" Dorcas's strident voice didn't halt Clara as much as the realization that Henry was already gone. "Let that *Englisher* go. Your mother ruined her life. I won't—"

Clara didn't let her finish. "You don't even know Henry. And you didn't know my father."

Dorcas stood on the porch, her brows raised. Maybe she was incredulous that Clara would speak like this. Clara had never done so before.

"If my mother hadn't met my father, I wouldn't be here." Clara's voice shook. She'd wanted to say the words for so long.

"And now your mother isn't here." Dorcas's lips pinched into a white line.

There was no arguing with her.

Clara stared at her, seeing an old woman who'd grown to be argumentative and judgmental. She wouldn't change her mind.

And what was the use? Henry had said his goodbyes.

Everything was muddled. Clara had started this whole thing because she'd wanted Dorcas to approve of her. She'd wanted to belong, at events where everyone was coupled off. She'd wanted to belong to a husband.

But the chasm between her and Dorcas was deeper than ever. And Clara had fallen for Henry, who didn't want her after all.

She was all alone.

Chapter Seventeen

"**W**here's Henry?"

Clara wanted to grit her teeth against the frustration of hearing that same question for the third time that night, but she forced a smile instead. The night air was cool, but inside the Troyers' barn where the singing was held, it was warm and full of chatter and bodies.

"I don't know," Clara told Trudy.

She'd given the same answer to Samantha and Robert, and neither one had asked follow-up questions.

But Trudy did. "It's weird to see you not together."

Clara swallowed. What was she supposed to say to that?

Every day without talking to Henry felt wrong.

"Abe brought me."

The singing was over now. Abe had picked her up in his buggy, and once they'd arrived, he'd joined some of his friends, which had left Clara adrift.

Until Trudy had seen her and come to her rescue.

She and Abe weren't a couple. He had only invited her to this singing.

But Clara couldn't help thinking that Henry would've stuck by her side. Henry would've mumbled the words to the old German songs and winked at her when her nerves got the best of her and gotten her a glass of lemonade after the singing was done.

Clara had to stop comparing Abe to Henry. It wasn't fair to Abe. Or to her heart.

Henry was special.

And he wasn't in her life any longer.

"I thought—" Trudy stumbled over the words. Smiled a chagrined smile. "I guess it doesn't matter what I thought if you and Henry aren't together."

Clara blinked against the sting of tears. "Maybe it's for the best," she whispered. "My great-aunt doesn't approve of Henry."

Trudy's expression showed compassion. "Because he's an *Englisher*?"

She nodded, her throat hot. "My father was an *Englisher*. My mother left the faith for him."

What had happened with her parents wasn't a secret. It had caused a big stir when it had occurred, but Trudy didn't seem shocked.

Trudy cleared her throat. "My *mamm* knows your *aendi*. She might've mentioned that she isn't the most forgiving person. Something about a grudge she'd held for years over a young man who'd come courting her sister instead of her."

"I didn't know that."

Trudy patted her arm. "Family can be difficult. Have you ever thought of moving out?"

Moving out?

"I—I don't think I can afford it."

But Clara's bank account balance had slowly been growing with the money she'd been able to set aside from her cleaning jobs. Lena had offered her a steady gig. Maybe someday.

Abe approached and Trudy greeted him. They chatted for a few moments while the thought ran through Clara's mind.

Clara wasn't in the same place she'd been two years ago when she'd arrived in Hickory Harbor. She'd been hollowed out with grief, had no money, no connections. Living with her great-aunt had been the only choice.

But now she had friends. Todd and Lena might write her a recommendation if she wanted to get an apartment.

She could live on her own. Make her own decisions.

The event wound down, and as Clara left the singing with Abe, the thought settled into a leaden ball in her stomach. Even if she lived on her own, it wouldn't change things with Henry.

Abe helped her into the buggy and they set off at a leisurely pace.

"Did you have a *goot* time tonight?" he asked.

"Yes." Clara was surprised to discover it was true. She'd thought things would be awkward—and they had been— but it had been a comfort to see the new friends she'd made.

She wasn't alone anymore.

An awkward silence fell between them.

Henry would've known what to say to break her out of the awkwardness. Maybe he would've commented on the line of buggies snaking its way out to the main road, where everyone would go their separate ways.

But Clara sat tongue-tied and wondering what Abe was thinking. What he might say next.

After what seemed like a long while, he tipped his head, his gaze landing on her face in the near dark. "I am not sure Micah was telling me the truth when he said things weren't serious between you and Henry."

She thought of Henry's serious expression that last evening. Tears pricked—again—but she was able to stave them off.

"I—I think I felt more for him than he did for me."

She didn't know how to go on with a broken heart. But maybe it was like a grieving heart. You had no choice but to keep living life, no matter how much it hurt.

Abe shook his head. "I saw the way he looked at you during practices."

A bolt of hope surged, and then just as quickly, a bolt of despair.

Clara shook her head. "You're mistaken. Henry doesn't feel—he doesn't—"

She couldn't say any more for the lump in her throat.

There was silence again for a few moments and then he said, "If there's hope for me, I'd like to see you again. Maybe we could go for a walk after house church on Sunday?"

Did she want that? She considered the awkward silences between them, the distance between them during the singing.

It wasn't fair to compare him to Henry, but her heart was, anyway.

Clara didn't feel an iota of what she felt for Henry when she was with Abe. Maybe it would come, in time.

But right now, her heart wasn't in a courtship with Abe.

"I think… I need some time."

Would her heart ever heal?

Henry sat in his truck the next morning, just after dawn.

The sun was rising behind him as he stared at the little house he'd spent weeks working on.

All for nothing.

He hadn't gotten a chance to finish.

It would take another week of work at least, all on his own. And Henry didn't have that.

He'd failed.

Not his father, but he'd failed himself.

There was a part of him that wanted to stay. Stick it out no matter what Dad said.

Henry got out of the truck and rounded to the tailgate. He'd brought a big cardboard box to collect Mama Kitty and her kittens.

But before he could reach for it, he noticed two buggies driving up the road. A couple of families heading to town?

Henry didn't have to wonder long. Both buggies turned into his drive.

He recognized Todd in the first buggy as he slowed the black horse and then brought it to a stop next to Henry's truck.

And was that...? It was David in the second buggy.

"What are you doing here?" he asked Todd when his brother had set the brake and climbed down from the buggy.

"Dad called me last night."

Henry's gut tightened. He crossed his arms over his chest. "I was gonna say goodbye before I left town."

David joined them. Henry had once felt frustration and a helpless anger toward his brother, and now he felt a brotherly affection.

"We thought you'd be here, working up until the end."

Henry's mouth twisted into a frown. "Guess you were both wrong. I'm done. Done trying to prove myself to Dad."

Todd watched him with a narrow-eyed stare. "I sorta thought you were trying to prove some things to yourself."

The truth of those words hit like a physical blow and Henry flared his nostrils as he exhaled slowly, trying to pretend it didn't hurt.

Todd's sharp gaze didn't miss anything. "You're not a failure simply because one job didn't get finished. Or because Nell turned out to be a different person than she'd pretended to be."

Henry knew that.

But there was a part of him that had wanted to prove that he was in a healthier headspace. That he could be depended on.

David seemed to follow his thoughts. "We can help you finish up here. It won't take long."

Henry shook his head. "Even with the three of us, there's too much to do…"

His voice trailed off, because behind David's buggy, two more buggies pulled in. These were packed with three guys each—friends from volleyball, Henry realized. Behind them, several men on bikes rode up.

The men in buggies started unloading tools.

When he looked back at his brothers, both of them were grinning at his utter confusion.

"What is this?"

"If you could finish the house, would you?" Todd asked.

"Of course." He'd been thinking about it only moments ago.

"We brought help," Todd said. As if a team of twelve men appearing was a normal thing.

"But why?" Henry couldn't seem to wrap his mind around it.

"Because they are your friends. And friends show up." Todd made it sound simple.

Henry's breath was caught somewhere behind his sternum. With this many hands…it might be possible.

He'd thought all along that he had to prove himself by doing the work himself.

But what if he'd been wrong?

The men had started gathering round. It was David who suggested, "You'll have to give us some direction. Tell us what you need done and put us to work."

Henry reached for his toolbox from the bed of his truck.

"Don't give the doc any kind of saw," called out a voice from the back of the crowd. Henry didn't recognize the man.

David and several other guys chortled.

Todd scowled playfully. "It was one wire. And it was an accident."

The laughter got louder.

Henry led the way into the house, his brain already working ahead to the projects that needed tackling first.

Henry left David in charge of a crew painting the master bedroom and put Todd and another guy, who his brother introduced as a master craftsman, on installing the trim and hardware in the kitchen.

This just might work.

Henry found himself working alongside Robert, installing cabinet doors in the kitchen. From here, he could hear the guys ribbing each other, asking about someone's sick kid.

Realization washed over him.

This sense of community had been missing from his life. If he'd had a close group of friends when his life had imploded, maybe Henry wouldn't have fallen as deeply as he had.

Or maybe he would've had someone to sit with him when he did fall.

They were making good progress when he went out to the truck to grab some water.

Henry rounded the house and sat on the porch to have his drink. Micah was on the roof, touching up the trim around the chimney, just above.

Two of the kittens bounded out of the crawl space toward Henry, sniffing his boot.

David opened the back door, a cup of paint and paintbrush in hand. He stayed in the doorway, touching up paint on the jamb.

Henry let the kittens sniff and watched as they went farther out into the grass.

"Friends of yours?"

Henry glanced up at his brother. "Not really. The mama gave birth here and I wanted to wait until the kittens were older before I took them away."

"Hmm." David took a long time considering the kitten playing with Henry's boot lace. "So you've been feeding them? Giving them water?"

And Henry had put a blanket inside the crawl space so Mama Kitty could keep them warm. It was right there in plain sight for David to see.

"We've got animal control in Hickory Harbor," David said. "Lots of farmers around here would've taken them in."

But the cats had mattered to Clara.

And maybe Henry had gotten a little attached.

"You should stay," David said.

When Henry glanced at him curiously, David laughed a little and rubbed the back of his neck. "Ruby told me I should tell you how I feel."

Warmth ignited in Henry's chest. His sister-in-law was something. "I can see her saying that."

"It's been...*goot*. Getting to know you. The girls love you."

Henry had gotten close to the two munchkins over the past weeks. He'd miss his brother—both of them—when he left.

"I don't know where I'm going to end up," he said honestly.

"My uncle doesn't have any sons. He's looking for someone young to eventually take over the business." Henry glanced up as Micah's voice called down off the roof.

David had a bit of a grin on his lips. "I'm not the only one who'd like it if you stayed."

Henry didn't know if he could do that. Not when Clara was courting with someone else—might eventually marry someone else.

But the idea had its merits. Henry had never experienced community like this before.

"You'd have to learn pneumatic tools," came Robert's voice from the roof again.

David nodded to the kittens. "Maybe there's a reason you didn't walk away from them."

Maybe David was reaching for straws.

But he was right about one thing.

Henry didn't want to leave.

Chapter Eighteen

Clara crashed to the ground, landing hard enough to knock the breath out of her. Her legs were pinned beneath the bike, and she waited a moment until her chest unlocked and she could draw a good breath.

"What are you doing?"

Dorcas's demanding voice turned Clara's head. The older woman was climbing down the porch steps.

Clara took a moment to catch her breath before she untangled her feet and skirts from the bicycle.

The skin on Clara's palms stung, and she was sweaty and now dusty from another fall.

But she didn't care.

"I'm going to ride this bike," she said to her great-aunt.

Dorcas stood on the bottom step and watched as Clara straddled the bike and then pushed off with her right foot steady on the pedal.

Clara only made it a few feet before the wobble in the front wheel threw her off balance and the bike crashed to the ground again.

This time, Clara hopped free and only the bike fell. She winced, anyway. The poor bike. How much abuse could it take?

"Who gave you that bike?"

Clara didn't bother answering the growled question. She'd kept the bike hidden all this time because she didn't want to answer questions about Henry or face Dorcas's criticism.

But that didn't matter now.

Clara missed Henry deeply. And after talking with Trudy and Abe last night, she'd realized that she would regret it for the rest of her life if she didn't fight for him— fight for their relationship.

Clara didn't know what it might look like. She was dedicated to the Amish church. And Henry was an *Englisher*. But if God meant for them to be together, He would provide a way. Wouldn't He?

She stood over the bike again, eyeing the flat grassy space. She was going to get it this time. She ignored the twist of fear in her belly and kicked off.

She made it farther than ever before, but then the front wheel of the bike must've hit a stone or something, because the wheel jerked in her hands. She lost her concentration and felt herself begin to fall.

This time, she tried to correct her balance.

Only she overcorrected and the bike crashed to the ground the other way. Clara didn't have time to move and felt the scrape on her shin as she became trapped under the bike. Again.

"Clara, you're being disrespectful."

Dorcas's voice set her teeth on edge. Time was running out. She needed to find Henry. She'd look at the construction site first, and if he'd already gone, she would go to Todd and Lena's and beg for his phone number and the chance to call him.

"How am I being disrespectful?" she asked patiently as she untangled herself and stood up again.

"You're ignoring me."

Had Clara been lost in her thoughts and missed something Dorcas had said? She didn't think so.

She lifted the bike again. Checked the tires. They looked all right. She didn't think she'd damaged it in the fall.

For a moment, Clara turned and looked directly at Dorcas, though she kept hold of the bike handlebars.

"I mean no disrespect to you," she said the words clearly. "But I miss Henry. I lo—I care about him."

Dorcas's face flushed and her eyes snapped. "That's why you're doing this? To see that *Englisher*?"

Clara nodded. "I don't even know whether he is still in Hickory Harbor, but I have to tell him how I feel."

Dorcas took a step off the porch. "I forbid it." She spat the words and Clara saw her hand shaking. "I forbid you to see that *Englisher* again."

Clara shook her head. "I am not a child. I will make my own decision on this."

Henry was a good man, a Godly man. Maybe they had begun their relationship as a pretense, but she knew him.

And she knew that being with him was right—if he would accept it.

Dorcas was spluttering. Her face had gone from pink to near purple. Clara had never seen her this angry before, and for one moment, she felt a beat of discomfort. What if Dorcas disowned her? Kicked her out of the house?

Clara would mourn the relationship. Try her best to reconnect with her great-aunt.

But Clara couldn't let fear dictate her life. Not any longer.

"Get off that bicycle," Dorcas hissed the words.

For the first time, Clara saw her clearly. She saw a lonely old woman who wanted things to be just so. There was no room for making mistakes here, no room to stretch and grow.

Clara had found the safe place she'd needed to land when her grandparents had passed away. Dorcas had taught her the Amish faith and introduced her to the Hickory Harbor community.

But Dorcas was also controlling and harsh.

Dorcas wouldn't change her mind about Henry.

And neither would Clara.

"No," Clara said gently. "I love you and I respect you. I do. But I won't relent on this. I belong with Henry. And I'm going to find him."

This time when Clara kicked off, something was different. Something inside her brain clicked into place and she felt the combination of momentum and balance. She pedaled for all she was worth and then she was riding.

Clara's heart pounded and then flew as she took off. She sped up gradually until she heard the air rushing past her ears.

And then a moment of panic as she tried to remember how to slow down and stop.

Clara was breathing hard when she eased her shaking feet from the pedals to the ground.

She'd made a large circle and ended up right where she'd started.

Dorcas was watching her with a horrified look on her face. "You're as stubborn as your mother." Dorcas's tone made it clear that it was not a compliment.

But Clara remembered her mother's warmth, her laugh, her faith.

And she smiled. "I'll be back later. I've got to find Henry."

The older woman called out something, but Clara couldn't make out the words as she kicked off again. There was a threatening wobble, but Clara pushed the pedals harder and momentum carried her forward.

She didn't fall.

She knew a moment of terror as she left the end of the driveway and turned her bike toward Henry's house. She wouldn't find him there, but it was the first place they'd met. And she might need to check on the cats.

After that, she'd track down Henry no matter what it took.

She was ready to give him her heart.

Henry was affixing the shutters on the outside windows on the front of the house when he heard a car pull up in the drive.

He put in two more nails with the pneumatic nail gun Micah had loaned him before leaning back to inspect his work. Beautiful.

Henry would need to touch up the paint where the nails had gone in, but it looked near perfect.

He lowered the nail gun and turned to see who'd arrived.

Only to find Mom and Dad climbing out of his father's work truck.

The noise level coming from the house had died down as project after project had been completed. Several guys had gone home as the afternoon waned, though Todd and David and a couple other guys remained, touching up the paint inside. Someone was running a Shop-Vac, likely cleaning up dust from the floors.

The house was coming together, and Henry felt a bolt of pride at what they'd accomplished today.

It made it easier to throw his shoulders back as he walked over to greet his parents.

"Hey." He kissed Mom's cheek, tried to warn her that he was sweaty and dirty.

She hugged him anyway.

"What's going on here?" Dad asked, his eyes on the house.

It looked so different from when Henry had sat in his truck this morning, filled with hurt and anger and despair.

"A few friends showed up to help," Henry said.

Dad wasn't really listening, his focus on the house. He absently wandered toward the door.

Henry was sure he would be back. Dad had told him to abandon the project and he hadn't. Surely Dad would say something about that.

"Do you want to see the inside?" he asked Mom. "David and Todd are around here somewhere."

The joy on Mom's face as he mentioned his brothers gave him a spike of warmth in his belly.

"In a bit," she said.

Henry moved back to where he'd left the nail gun and unhooked it from the air line so he could wind up the hose. "Dad looks good."

It was true. Henry saw better color in his father's face, less stress lines around his mouth.

"He had a good doctor's visit last week," Mom said. "The doctor seems to think selling the business will reduce his stress."

"I hope so."

Henry finished coiling the hose and saw Mom's head tip to the side. "You seem...less stressed."

He smiled at her. "I'll apologize to him later. I'm sure he told you I bit his head off last time we talked."

Henry tucked the coiled hose behind the air compressor and straightened.

She was still considering him. "You seem more settled."

Henry didn't know about that. There was still a Clara-shaped hole in his heart.

Mom wasn't finished. "I spoke to Nell."

He waited for the familiar cut, the humiliation and shame to wash over him.

It didn't come.

Mom looked chagrined. "She called me and I couldn't stop thinking about you and Clara. I tried to be gentle and tell her that I didn't think it was appropriate for us to speak so often."

Oh.

He put his arm around Mom's shoulders. "I can only imagine how she took it."

Mom shook her head, laughing a stunned little laugh. "I honestly didn't know. And I'm sorry."

He figured Nell had probably unleashed her vitriol on Mom, who would never deserve that. "I'm sorry." He should've done something to keep Nell from contacting Mom in the first place.

Mom stepped back and now he noticed the shine of tears in her eyes. She sniffed. "She let something slip. Something that you never told me. That she'd cheated."

He felt the pulse of the old hurt, but weak now. A wound that was healed.

"I didn't know how to tell you," he said. "Didn't want you to know."

He saw Mom's composure crack. "I wish you could've trusted me—trusted your father and me with this."

Henry shook his head slightly. "It wasn't about trust. It was about me, not wanting you to know what a failure I'd been. I wasn't enough to keep her attention, keep her love."

"Oh, Henry." He folded Mom into his arms when she looked like she needed a hug. But she was quick to push back with a fierce look on her face. "You are an incredible man. The problem was with her, never with you."

He couldn't help smiling at her ferocity. "I know," he said gently. "It just took me a while to get there."

"It's because of Clara." Now he felt the pain he'd expected earlier.

"Mom, there's something you should know." This was difficult. "Clara and I—well, we faked that we were dating."

His mom's sharp eyes missed nothing as she scoured his face. "What?"

Henry felt entirely sheepish as he admitted, "I wanted to prove to you that I was over Nell. Maybe keep you from trying to push us back together. I should've just told you the truth."

"I don't believe it," she said finally. "You're not that good an actor."

"Believe it. Clara agreed to help me because she wanted dating lessons—she wants an Amish husband."

Mom shook her head. "Clara has strong feelings for you. I know it."

He remembered staring at Clara's tear-filled eyes two days ago, when he'd gone to say goodbye. Maybe she did have feelings for him, but they weren't big enough to change her life plan, or to go against her aunt.

"She wants to belong here, in Hickory Harbor." The words burned his throat. "I can't give her that."

Now Mom's brows rose in incredulity. "You don't think so? Not even after your brothers and your friends have helped you do this?" She waved her hand to encompass the whole house.

The words opened an idea inside him. One he hadn't allowed himself to consider before now.

Todd had relocated to Hickory Harbor. He'd joined the Amish church and was content and fulfilled. He was a pillar in the community.

Why couldn't Henry do the same?

His dad exited the house before the idea could really solidify.

Mom gave Henry one more pointed looked and murmured, "I'd better say hi to your brothers."

Henry bent to pick up a jar of putty so he could fill the holes in the shutters the nail gun had left behind.

"You didn't have to do this," Dad said. "Patterson would've finished the build."

"I know." But Henry felt the pride of a job well done. He'd done what he came here to do.

"The house looks amazing. Patterson would be lucky to have you join his team as one of the foremen."

Henry used a putty knife to fill holes. "I'll talk to him, but I don't know where I'm gonna end up, Dad. Maybe it's time I go into business for myself."

Dad was quiet and Henry stopped working to look over at him.

"I'm healing," Henry told his father. "It's been a long road, but the demons that were chasing me when I failed you on the Dudley project are behind me now."

Was Henry seeing things? Dad's eyes looked a little shiny. "I've only ever wanted the best for you, son."

Henry's throat grew hot. "I know."

"I'm proud of you."

Henry didn't need the words. But they covered the old wound inside him, the shame that had told him he had failed his dad.

He moved forward, or maybe Dad did, and then they were embracing.

Henry laughed breathlessly as Dad let him go with one more back slap. "Thanks for sending me to Hickory Harbor."

He'd meant to say more, but lost focus as he caught sight of someone wobbling up the driveway on a bike.

Chapter Nineteen

Clara had felt confident out on the wide shoulder of the road, but there were buggies and horses and two trucks in Henry's drive, and as she slowed down, her confidence waned and she began to wobble.

But Henry was on the porch, and as Clara concentrated on not smashing into the doctor's buggy, he stepped off the porch and then began jogging toward her.

Her heart leaped. Henry!

She slowed and the wobble in her wheels grew more pronounced but he was there, catching the handlebars in his big hands.

Henry was here. Only now did she let the realization flow over her. He hadn't gone yet.

"You're still here," she breathed.

"And you're riding a bike." There was a smile in his voice. And it was quickly followed by curiosity. "What are you doing here?"

"I needed to see you—"

"Hi, Clara," Todd said as he passed by where she and Henry stood staring at each other.

The greeting broke through her focused thoughts and she felt a blush rising in her face as she murmured a return hello. It seemed as if everyone was packing up, carting tools to the buggies and trucks parked in the drive.

Henry's mother and father were on the porch. Clara got off the bike as they approached.

"Here," Henry took the bike out of her hands, moving it to lean against the tailgate of his truck.

"How are you, dear?"

Clara accepted the hug from Kimberly. "I'm all right. What about you?"

"Fine, fine." Kimberly seemed to have something stuck in her eye. Or maybe she was trying to send Henry a signal, because her wide eyes seemed to be pointed at him.

"Bye, Mom," Henry said with a sigh.

"C'mon, Kimberly." Michael ushered her toward the truck at the end of the drive.

"I'll call you tomorrow," Henry said to his dad.

Clara waved and when she turned back to Henry, he was staring at her hand. She turned the appendage and saw the angry scrape on her palm. Most of the blood had dried but the wound was still raw and pink.

"I might've fallen a couple of times," she admitted.

"I've got a first aid kit in the truck." He tipped his head and she followed him to the truck, then around the side of the house where it was quieter.

Henry nodded to the stoop and it was the perfect height for her to sit. He knelt in front of her, opening the plastic box on the cement slab beside her.

His head was bowed as he rifled through the contents of the first aid kit and her heart swelled with love.

Clara had her hand resting on her thigh, palm upward. He reached for her and gently took her other hand, the one fisted beside her skirt, and turned it up to face him.

The scrape on that palm was just as bad as the one on her right hand.

"How many times did you fall?" There was a teasing lilt to his voice.

"A few. Until I finally figured out how to balance and pedal at the same time."

Henry smiled up at her and the words caught behind her throat. Clara stared at his bowed head as he gently dabbed her palms with antiseptic. His touch was gentle and sure.

Just tell him.

"I missed you," she whispered.

"Yeah?" His head tipped and she saw the serious, steady gaze.

"I'm—I'm sorry about my great-aunt. She shouldn't have said the things she said." Clara took a deep breath. He was concentrating on doctoring her hands. "And I should've said something to her before."

Henry squeezed her hand gently, though he hadn't looked up yet. She stared at the hair that was just a little too long, curling over his collar in the back.

Everything was there, on her baited breath. *I love you. I want to be with you.*

But her gaze moved past Henry to where the cat sat just outside her hole, licking one paw.

"I spoke to Dorcas this morning." It was easier to start this way. "I told her that I couldn't keep letting her dictate my life."

Something was bothering Clara.

Henry hummed, still working on applying a bandage on her palm while she tried to figure out what was wrong.

Then it hit her.

The kittens were nowhere in sight.

"Where are the kittens?"

Henry glanced over his shoulder and then back to Clara, a slight smile on his face. "They were big enough to find homes of their own. Turns out David wanted one for his girls, and Micah and Robert took one each."

He sounded happy.

But all she could think was, *he's given them up because he's leaving.*

Uncertainty swamped her.

What if Henry was humoring her? Listening because he'd been a good friend, not because he harbored any romantic feelings toward her?

She was only Clara. A nobody with only a grumpy old aunt and maybe nowhere to go home to.

"There." Henry pressed the last bandage to her palm.

He closed the box and then sat back on his heels to look her in the face.

It was a risk to tell him her feelings. Clara might be hurt.

But if she didn't take the chance, if she didn't tell him, she would regret it for the rest of her life.

She had to take the chance.

Before she could say anything, the cat stalked out from her hole and came to butt against Henry's knee. He chuckled and scratched her head.

She caught sight of the water bowl and blanket Henry had given to the cat. A man who had a tender heart for a stray cat was someone she could trust with her heart.

She reached out her hand and Henry took it and drew her to her feet.

Henry's hope was soaring.

Clara was here.

His mom's words came back to him. *Clara has strong feelings for you. I know it.*

But she looked uncertain and one corner of her mouth was pulled in like she was chewing on the inside of her lip.

"I'm so glad you're here," he said. Tenderness was probably leaking out from every pore and she seemed to respond to it, her eyes softening.

"You are?"

"Yeah. I was probably going to come to you." He hadn't made up his mind until the moment he'd seen her again. His brave girl, riding the bike that had terrified her before.

Henry clasped both of her hands in his. He wanted her closer but he was aware of at least two people moving around inside. Probably David and Todd finishing the cleanup. He didn't want to do anything to embarrass Clara.

So he settled for simply holding her hands.

"What were you going to say?" Clara asked.

She'd been brave enough to ride that bike over here. It was his turn to find some courage.

"What I should've said the other day. I was scared."

The words weren't as difficult to say as Henry had thought they might be.

"You were?" She looked shocked. "Scared of me?"

"Scared that you'd see the real me. You'd see what everyone else sees and... I let you go before you could send me away when that happened."

"Henry," she breathed. "How could you think that?"

He smiled wryly. "I thought I could save myself from the hurt. But it didn't work."

"It didn't?"

"No. Clara, I've missed you like a part of myself was missing. I haven't slept. I can't stop thinking about you."

A single silver tear slipped down her cheek and Henry dropped her hands to cup her face, brushing that tear from her cheek with his thumb.

"I missed you, too." Clara's soft admission hitched, as if she was holding back more tears.

He tipped his head so that his forehead gently touched hers. "Clara—"

His intention had been to kiss her. Her lips were right there and he wanted to reassure her, comfort her—

The back door opened. Clara jumped.

Henry edged back and dropped his hands, turning his body so that she was mostly blocked from sight.

It was Todd standing with one foot out the door, a pleased grin lurking on his mouth. "Just letting you know we finished up here. You want me to lock the door on my way out?"

Henry shook his head. "I'll get it."

Todd hesitated, then said, "Come over later, if you want to talk."

Henry did want to talk. He wanted to know how his brother had really felt when he'd left his *Englisher* life behind and was it hard to adapt to living Amish. Henry had learned about the Amish faith by attending worship with his brother, but he needed to know more. Everything had changed today.

"Bye, Clara," Todd called out gently.

Clara whispered a goodbye and Todd winked at Henry before he moved to go back through the house.

"Wait—" Henry took a step toward his brother, who stopped on the threshold. "Thank you. For everything." For writing all those letters when Todd had first decided to move to Hickory Harbor. For pulling him into the family when Henry would've backed away. For showing up today.

Todd knew. He smiled. "That's what brothers are for."

And then he was gone and Henry spun around to face

Clara. She was looking at him with warmth shining from her eyes. "You finished the house."

"Thanks to my brothers. And my friends." He took a half step closer, but he wasn't touching her. Not yet. "I never expected...this." He waved his hand behind him to encompass the house. "For them to show up. Practically twist my arm to work today. Help was here, even when I didn't know. I just had to ask for it."

More tears brimmed in her eyes. "I'm glad for you." Clara's voice trembled, though. There was still something she was worrying about. "Are you—will you still go back to Columbus?"

Henry motioned toward the cat, who was now stretching out in the grass, lying on her side in the waning sunlight.

"Mama Kitty needs a place to stay. And so do I."

Her bottom lip trembled. "You're keeping her?"

He groaned, unable to resist having her closer when she was so emotional. Henry reached for her and she came easily into his arms. Holding her was right.

Her nose pressed against his neck as he cupped the back of her head. "I'm keeping the cat. And I'm staying in Hickory Harbor. I want to come courting—not pretend anymore."

Clara leaned back slightly in his arms so he had a clear view of her face. Her eyes were searching, like she couldn't believe what he was saying.

He brushed a finger over the softness of her cheek. "I love you, Clara. You are so precious to me. I can't promise I won't ever get scared again, but I'm here to stay. If you'll have me."

A little laugh-sob hiccupped out of her. Her smile was beaming. "Henry, I love you. I was scared to say it but I want us to be together."

He didn't need to hear anything more. He dipped his head and captured her lips with his.

Henry poured all of his love and hope and apology and promise into the kiss.

She met each touch sweetly and both of them were breathless when he pulled away from the kiss and folded her close in his arms.

"My great-aunt will be furious," she whispered into his shoulder.

Henry squeezed her gently. "We'll go and talk to her together. You're not alone. Not anymore."

A shudder went through Clara at his words and then she relaxed fully into his arms.

He would protect her—as much as he could—from her aunt's ire and sharp words.

"Maybe she'll relent when we get married—eventually."

Clara gasped softly and leaned back in his arms, her eyes wide.

He smiled gently at her. "I'm in this forever, Clara. I want to be your family. For us to belong to each other—and to our community here."

She nodded, choked up so that words wouldn't come. But her beaming smile told him enough.

Henry folded her close again, turning them so that they could look at the house.

Maybe he'd buy it. The thought pinged into his brain and settled.

This house was the first place he'd met Clara. It had brought him to Hickory Harbor. He'd put weeks of work into it, crafted it with his own hands.

It would be a great place to raise a family.

He'd bring that up much later.

Henry didn't know what the future would hold. There

were still things that needed to be worked out. A job for him. Clara's relationship with her aunt. Whether he would join the Amish faith.

But he knew that God had brought him here and that he was home.

Chapter Twenty

18 months later...

*G*runt.

Slap.

"That was a foul and you know it."

Henry breathed in shallow bursts as he spun on the drive-way, dribbling the basketball.

Todd stepped in front of Henry, arms wide. "No way." He was just as breathless as Henry.

Todd tried to block, but Henry put up a pretty bank shot and the ball slipped through the net with a *whuff.*

Todd scowled. "Tied up." He tossed the ball to Henry. "Check."

Henry bounce-passed it back, then dropped into a squat, waiting for his brother's first move.

It was Saturday morning, eighteen months after his broth-ers had showed up and set him straight at the job site. Henry and Todd had a standing appointment every other Saturday morning to play basketball together and catch up.

On this spring morning, a warm weather pattern had brought a wave of humidity and the back of Henry's shirt was soaked with sweat.

But he wouldn't have it any other way.

"How's Jimmy?" Todd asked, dribbling backward and then taking a three-point shot that bounced off the backboard and almost right back into his hands.

"We had a talk last week and it seems to have helped—for now."

This time when Todd took a shot, Henry blocked it. The ball bounced off the driveway and into the grass between the barn and house.

Henry jogged to get it.

The police had found the young man who'd vandalized the job site. Jimmy was a fourteen-year-old with an attitude problem who'd lost his dad two years before. Henry's house wasn't the only one he'd vandalized, and a judge had offered the boy a choice between juvie and community service hours, if he could find someone who'd work with him.

After praying and talking with Clara about it, Henry had taken the boy on. Jimmy had been obnoxious and angry for the first two weeks they'd worked together. It had taken every last ounce of Henry's patience to deal with the boy—and it had paid off.

Jimmy had slowly warmed up, begun to share about himself, begun to trust Henry. Now he worked for Henry fifteen hours a week and they had grown close.

Sometimes Jimmy reverted to past behavior patterns. A few weeks ago, Henry had caught him slacking off on the job and upset. They'd talked and Henry had given him advice.

He enjoyed being a "big brother" to the younger guy.

"Have you spoken to Dad this week?" Todd asked just before he stole the ball from Henry, who took off after him.

"Yeah. He and Mom are heading out in their camper for a weeklong trip around the state."

Todd's eyes met his for a second before he took an easy layup.

"He gave me some advice on the job I'm doing for Eli Glick."

Henry's relationship with Dad had smoothed out in the months after Dad had sold the company. They'd cleared the air about what had happened when Henry had gone through his breakup with Nell.

Dad had been vital in advising Henry on establishing his own contracting business here in Hickory Harbor. Henry worked with Amish and *Englisher* families alike and he'd flourished managing his own company. Everything from bidding on jobs to scheduling them, working with his hands and learning new tools and ways of doing things satisfied him. But there was nothing quite like the feeling of pride he experienced when he welcomed a family into their new or renovated home.

It was nice that Dad was proud of him. Henry was proud of himself, of what he'd accomplished.

And Henry had promised to open up to his parents when things were going on in his life. Their relationship was stronger than ever.

And it helped that both Dad and Mom loved Clara.

"Are you two about finished? Lunch is ready. David and Ruby will be here any minute!"

Speaking of Clara.

He grabbed the ball between both hands and turned to face the porch where Clara was standing next to Lena, watching them. Clara was shielding her eyes, and even from here, he could see the smile lingering around her mouth.

He also couldn't miss the baby bump that stood out under Clara's dress. They'd been married for fourteen months and he'd never dreamed that God had this in store for him. A visceral happiness gripped him, a familiar one that came over him often when he glimpsed his wife.

How was this his life? He was blessed beyond measure.

Todd poked the ball from behind Henry's arm. It bounced on the ground and Todd moved around him to scoop it up.

"C'mon. One more point," Todd said. "Stop making doe eyes at your wife."

"For the win," Henry agreed. He put himself between his brother and the basketball net. "And I don't even know what doe eyes are."

Todd laughed and took a long shot before Henry could defend him. "I don't either. Lena read it in a book once and showed it to me."

Henry dribbled the ball and tried to push past his brother, but Todd planted his feet and Henry was forced to whirl and go around him.

Henry's shot clanged off the rim. Right into Todd's hands.

Todd grinned. "C'mon, little bro. Don't let me win."

Henry took it up a notch as he defended the goal from his brother.

This. He felt such a beat of happiness as it thrummed in his blood that he missed a step and Todd took the shot.

It went in, and Todd raised his arms in victory.

Henry didn't care. He had gained a deeper friendship with his brother, a relationship he'd thought was broken beyond repair.

He'd grown closer to David, too. His nieces and nephew were special and he and Clara spent time with them nearly every week.

"You're not upset I won?" Todd asked.

"Nah." Henry fell into step beside his brother as they

walked toward the house and their waiting wives. "Just dwelling on the overflowing blessings in my life."

"Oh, yeah?"

"Yeah."

"Well, let me give you one more," Todd said.

Henry glanced over at his brother, who wore a secretive smile.

"You can't tell anyone," Todd said. "Yet."

Henry looked to make sure they were still out of earshot from the ladies. Probably.

Henry nodded.

"Lena's expecting. She's due a few months after Clara."

Joy rolled through Henry and he threw his arm around his brother's sweaty shoulders. "Congratulations!"

When he pulled away, he caught Lena rolling her eyes at her husband. Had she guessed he'd told?

Todd's grin was even wider than before.

Lena leaned over and said something low to Clara, who embraced her quickly.

"She'll be mad at me for spilling the beans," Todd said. "She wanted to wait, but I couldn't keep it from you. I'm so thankful God restored our relationship."

Henry couldn't hold back and gave his brother a real hug, one that the moment deserved.

He caught Clara's stare from over Todd's shoulder, watched a happy tear streak down her face.

He couldn't have known when God brought Clara into his life just how much she would change him—but he wouldn't have it any other way.

"*Aendi* Clara! Look!"

Clara turned at the kitchen counter to find Mindy at her elbow, pointing to the cookie sheet where she'd lined up chocolate chip cookie dough in haphazard lines. The cookie dough was misshapen and needed evening out but Mindy's earnest expression made Clara smile.

"Look what you did. Good work! I can't wait to taste them."

Ruby was cleaning up the mess of flour and butter smeared into the far end of the kitchen counter. Over Mindy's head, she shook her head with a tender smile.

Someone tugged on Clara's skirt and she looked down to see Timothy there. The tot raised his arms. "Lif' me up!"

"Timothy, no—"

"It's all right," Clara reassured Ruby. "He's not too heavy for me."

It was a little awkward holding Timothy to her hip with the baby bump in the way, but the boy's gurgle of delight was worth it.

"Mo' tookies!" Timothy shrieked.

The little boy had begun to speak early—coached by his sisters—and was just as loud as Maggie had been at two.

Clara tickled under Timothy's chin. "No more cookies. Maybe next time."

She adored spending time with Henry's nieces and nephew, whether it was baking or helping Mindy with her schoolwork or plain old babysitting. Ruby had become a close friend.

Ruby had suspected Clara was pregnant before anyone else and had quietly suggested some remedies, like a home-made ginger candy that had helped with morning sickness in the beginning. Ruby and Lena had been Clara's confidants when she confessed she wasn't sure she knew how to be a good mother. Ruby had admitted that she had felt the same when she'd married David and Mindy had experienced some challenging behaviors. Lena had told Clara that she'd seen plenty of mothers of all different types during her work at the birthing center, and that Clara had good instincts. Both women had told her to trust herself and lean on Henry.

Clara was so thankful to have two wonderful sisters-in-law. And the rest of Henry's family that had folded her in and welcomed her.

"Are you bugging *Aendi* Clara?" Lena swept into the kitchen behind Clara and tugged a happy Timothy into her arms.

Lena still looked a little peaked and Clara felt both a deep happiness for her friend and a pang of empathy. Lena had been excited to share the secret news that she and Todd were expecting.

"Mo' tookies!" Timothy shrieked again.

Lena danced him around the kitchen. "No. No more cookies for little boys." She sent a curious look to Clara. "But maybe for grown-up girls…?"

Clara laughed and nodded a little. "The bakery wants to add another flavor to their weekly order."

Ruby squealed in excitement and Lena cried, "Woo-hoo!"

Clara let the excitement of the moment—and having someone to celebrate with—wash over her. She'd begun baking cookies for the local bakery on a trial basis six months ago. Chocolate chip only. Six weeks into their trial period, the bakery owner had asked her for more cookies and a second flavor.

Six months later, Clara was baking twice a week and Henry was talking about modifying the kitchen to add a second oven.

And Clara was writing her second recipe book, this one already contracted by a local publisher.

Clara had never dreamed that her baking would become

a source of income or that she'd get to do something she loved to help support her family.

"What's all this fuss in here?" Kimberly joined the women and girls in the kitchen.

The room was bursting with family and Clara loved it.

"Are we celebrating the bakery news?" Kimberly asked. "Henry just told me. How exciting."

The moment was rich and full, but for a moment Clara experienced a pang of grief. She would have loved to celebrate this with Great-Aunt Dorcas.

The woman who had taken her in had never really warmed up to Henry, not even after he'd made the personal decision to join the Amish church. Dorcas had eventually forgiven Clara for what she'd seen as disrespect and ungratefulness.

Two weeks after the break in their relationship had been healed, Dorcas had passed away peacefully in her sleep. Clara was grateful for the time they'd been able to spend together, even though her great-aunt hadn't been as warm and caring as Clara had wanted.

Clara stood back for a moment as Ruby leaned down to say something to a chattering Mindy and watched Lena dance a gurgling, laughing Timothy around the room. Kimberly joined in.

And Clara was a part of it all. This was her family now, these *wonderbarr* women that God had brought into her life through Henry.

Her husband came into the kitchen behind her and then the room really was too full, the press of bodies too much.

"Let me steal you away for a minute," Henry whispered into her hair.

Clara took his hand and followed him outside onto the back porch.

The sun was high and the scene was idyllic with the small

farm behind them blooming and green in springtime. Henry came behind her and wrapped his arms around her waist. His jaw brushed her temple.

"You feeling all right? I wanted to make sure you weren't too tired after playing with the little girls all afternoon."

"I feel fine. What about you? I saw you get a hard elbow from your brother playing basketball."

He chuffed a little laugh in her hair. "I'm fine. I can still mop the floor with him."

She touched her belly and Henry's hand came to rest over hers. He laced their fingers together.

The little one inside her gave a kick, the movement a thump against her palm. Henry must've felt it, too, because suddenly he was holding his breath.

"I think she wants to be a basketball player, too." His voice was a murmur in her hair, filled with wonder.

"It could be a *he*."

"Could be."

She turned her face slightly so she could see him. "I can't wait to meet him or her. I hope the baby has your eyes."

Henry's eyes were soft now, a deep and abiding love shining through them.

She settled against him again, her head on his shoulder.

Two years ago, she never could have imagined this life. A husband who loved her, a baby on the way, an extended family that she adored.

Henry had come to her with his unconventional plan to fake date—and God had had a better plan in mind the whole time.

She was so thankful that God had put Henry in her life and given her all the dreams of her heart.

* * * * *

*If you liked this story from Lucy Bayer,
check out her previous Love Inspired books:*

A Convenient Amish Bride
Their Forbidden Amish Match

Available now from Love Inspired!

*Find more great reads at
www.LoveInspired.com.*

Dear Reader,

Thank you for reading this book. Henry and Clara both had to learn to see who they truly were to find their happy ending. I think that every person has a chance to have a similar journey. Discovering new facets of ourselves can be so tough—but so rewarding. What is the most inspiring thing you have discovered about yourself lately? I hope you see God's hand working in your life today and every day. God bless and thank you for reading.

Lucy Bayer